PURPOSEFUL PARENTING

KANCHAN THAKUR

Contents

Preface

Being a parent is a path full of love, challenges, happiness, and growth. In some ways, it is the most gratifying and hard job we can have. We learn as much about ourselves as we do about our kids from the new things that happen every day. The idea for this book came from wanting to share thoughts, stories, and useful tips to help parents handle this wonderful trip with trust and kindness. It is important to stop and think about what really means in a world where parenting is getting harder because of changing social norms, different cultural influences, and the fast growth of technology. Our goal with this book is to give a balanced view that takes into account both the traditional values of caring for children and being strict with them, as well as the need to be flexible in order to raise kids in today's world. We want to talk about the different stages of a child's growth, from birth to adolescence, pointing out common problems and giving good ways to help kids become emotionally strong, independent, and kind. This book is a helpful resource for parents from all walks of life. It is based on study, the experiences of other parents, and the opinions of experts. This book is for parents, whether you are a new parent or an old one. It is a sign that you are not going through this trip by yourself. Being a parent is not about being perfect; it is about making progress and building a strong bond with your kids. We hope that these pages will help you, reassure you, and give you ideas on how to enjoy every moment of being a parent with love and care.

Acknowledgements

I would want to express my great gratitude to the Almighty God for bestowing upon me the honour of motherhood and enabling me to go through the profound and life-altering adventure of being a parent. I can honestly say that this role has been an emotional roller coaster for me; it has been filled with happiness, growth, and innumerable moments that I will never forget.

I would want to express my deepest gratitude to my cherished son, Rana Pratap Singh. Even though it is commonly believed that a mother is her child's first teacher, he has been my most significant mentor from the very beginning of my child's life. Almost from the minute I found out about his arrival, he has imparted upon me a multitude of valuable lessons, altering my viewpoint and imbuing my life with a more profound sense of purpose.

I had a rebirth on the day that he was born, and it was the beginning of changes that have made me a better person in ways that I could not have anticipated. I would want to express my gratitude to Rana Pratap for the unending joy, laughter, and blessings that you constantly bring into my life. I am thankful for each and every moment that we spend together, and I consider it a great blessing to be able to travel this path with you as my compass and my source of motivation.

I
Understanding Your Parenting Philosophy

Many people think that becoming a parent is a natural step in life and a role that we naturally take on when we have kids. But to parent with intention, you have to change your mindset. You have to stop reacting to the day-to-day challenges of raising kids and start shaping the kind of parent you want to be and the kind of kids you want to raise. This chapter goes into detail about how to understand and define your own parenting philosophy. This will guide all of your decisions, actions, and interactions with your kids.

A Fresh Perspective on Parenting

People have traditionally thought of parenting as a duty: you have to take care of your kids, make sure they are safe, and help them through the important times in their lives. These things are undeniably important, but purposeful parenting pushes us to go even further. It makes us think about how the choices we make as parents will affect not only our children but also the people they will become and the legacy they will leave behind.

In this new way of thinking, parenting isn't just about taking care of kids; it's also about making adults who are strong, caring, resilient, and thoughtful. It means teaching kids values, building on their strengths, and making sure they have a safe, loving place to explore their abilities. Being proactive instead of reactive, reflective instead of impulsive, and deliberate instead of accidental are all parts of purposeful parenting.

Defining Your Parenting Philosophy

Your parenting philosophy is the set of beliefs and rules that guide how you act as a parent. It is a personalised plan for how to raise your children based on your values, goals, and aspirations. Understanding and talking about this philosophy is the first step towards purposeful parenting.

Before you start, think about some basic questions:

- **What type of parent do I want to be?** Think about the good qualities you admire in other people and the ones you want to have yourself. Are you trying to be kind, patient, confident, or willing to listen?
- **What kind of adults do I want my kids to become?** Imagine the traits you want your kids to develop as they grow up, such as independence, kindness, toughness, or creativity.
- **What values are the most important to me?** Think about what values you want your kids to learn from you. This could include honesty, kindness, respect, or a strong work ethic.
- **How does my culture, faith, or personal experiences affect the way I raise my children?** Your background and experiences will always affect how you raise your children. Think about how these things have affected your philosophy.
- By answering these questions, you can start to make a clear outline of your parenting philosophy. While you grow up and learn more about yourself, your kids, and the world around you, this philosophy doesn't have to stay the same. It can change as you do.

Defining Your Parenting Philosophy

Recognising that each child is different is a key part of purposeful parenting. It's possible that what works for one child might not work for another, and what works for one family might not work for yours. Accepting that each child is different means making sure that your parenting style is flexible, allowing for growth and change.

It's important to remember that your kids are unique people with their own personalities, skills, limitations, and goals. Making sure your child grows up in a way that respects their uniqueness and fits with your family's values is an important part of purposeful parenting.

The Significance of Intentional Parenting

When you are an intentional parent, you create a home where kids can feel safe, valued, and understood. They learn not only from what you say, but also from how you live your life. The way you act, think, and interact with others sets a strong example for them to follow.

Intentional parenting helps kids build a strong sense of who they are, emotional intelligence, and the ability to deal with life's problems. It gives them the skills they need to grow up to be successful, well-rounded adults who do good things for society.

Having a clear philosophy about parenting also gives you a sense of purpose and security. It takes away the stress and confusion that often come with parenting decisions because your choices are based on your core beliefs and principles.

Final Thoughts

To understand your parenting philosophy, you need to take a step back from the day-to-day tasks of parenting and think about the bigger picture. Instead of reacting, you have to become proactive, making decisions with clear goals in mind for each one. Keep in mind that your philosophy can change as you go along this path. Your family should be able to change it as you and your kids grow, learn, and adapt. As an intentional parent, you promise to care for your children with thought, love, and awareness throughout their lives, making sure that they are not only ready for life's challenges but also given the tools to thrive.

II
Establishing Values and Priorities for Your Family

As you begin the journey of intentional parenting, it is essential to define a core set of principles and priorities that will guide your family life. These principles serve as the guiding compass for your parenting choices and the foundation upon which your children will build their lives. This chapter will explore the importance of establishing these principles and priorities, as well as how to effortlessly incorporate them into your daily routines through concrete examples.

The Importance of Family Values

Family values represent the core beliefs and principles that shape your family's interactions, choices, and overall lifestyle. They define what is of paramount significance to your family, be it compassion, integrity, authenticity, diligence, or any other value you hold dear. Defining clear values provides consistency and stability in your parenting, helping your children understand what is expected of them and what they can expect from you.

For example, when integrity is a core value within your family, it indicates that honesty is not merely encouraged but expected in every situation. When a child admits to a mistake, rather than imposing severe consequences, consider praising their honesty and initiating a conversation about how they can avoid similar errors moving forward. This underscores the importance of integrity while simultaneously fostering a sense of accountability.

Establishing Your Family's Core Principles

The first step in defining family values is to clarify what is most important to you and your partner. This process involves reflecting on your own upbringing, experiences, and beliefs, while also engaging in discussions with your partner to reach a mutual understanding. Consider the following steps to assist you in articulating your family's values:

1. **Contemplate Your Early Years:** Reflect on the values that were emphasised in your family during your early years. What aspects did you find admirable, and in what ways would you choose to take a different approach with your children?

2. **Engage in Dialogue with Your Partner:** Begin an open conversation with your partner about the values that you both consider important. This dialogue ought to embody a spirit of compromise and empathy, as the insights from both perspectives will significantly influence the values of your family.

3. **Prioritise Your Values:** While many values are significant, trying to highlight too many at once can lead to a sense of overwhelm. Determine the five core values that you aspire to emphasise within your family.

4. **Engage Your Children:** Depending on their age, consider involving your children in this process by asking them about the values they find most important. This can cultivate a deeper bond with the family's values and elevate their drive to maintain them.

For example, let us consider a scenario where you and your partner determine that compassion, respect, and perseverance stand as your foremost family values. Thereafter, you clarify these values to your children, exploring the significance of each and how they can incorporate them into their everyday lives.

Incorporating Values into Everyday Living

After establishing your family's core principles, the next step is to weave them into your daily routines and interactions. This process involves demonstrating these values, providing opportunities for your children to embrace them, and strengthening their understanding through positive reinforcement and meaningful conversation.

1. Demonstrating Values: Children learn more from your actions than from your words. When compassion is a cherished family value, it should be demonstrated through your actions—be it by extending courtesy to strangers, assisting a neighbour in need, or offering kind words to those within your home. Your children will witness these behaviours and understand that compassion transcends mere concept; it embodies a way of life.

Example: In the midst of your supermarket visit, upon noticing the cashier's stress, you may choose to pause and sincerely express your gratitude for their commitment. Thereafter, you may explain to your child the importance of showing compassion, particularly when others are encountering difficulties.

2. Creating Opportunities: Offer your children pathways to embody and practise your family's values. This may involve daily responsibilities, community involvement, or fostering an environment where they support one another at home.

Example: When perseverance is a valued trait, encourage your child to remain steadfast in the face of demanding tasks, such as tackling a challenging homework assignment or mastering a new skill. Honour their hard work and advancement regardless of the results to highlight the significance of perseverance.

3. Reinforcing Values: Utilise positive reinforcement to recognise and commend your children when they embody the family's values. This may be achieved through verbal praise, incentives, or by articulating your pride in their behaviour.

Example: When your child exhibits respect by listening attentively while someone else is speaking, you might say, "I noticed how you listened to your friend without interrupting." Your respectfulness is commendable, and I appreciate it greatly.

4. Family Dialogues: Engage in regular discussions about your family's values, tailored to be age-appropriate for your children. Leverage common situations as educational moments to strengthen these principles.

During family meals, consider bringing up a situation that arose that day—such as a disagreement at school—and discuss how your family's values of respect and compassion can be utilised to address such conflicts.

Focusing on What is Most Important
In addition to defining values, intentional parenting also involves setting priorities. Values relate to the way you conduct your life, whereas priorities focus on where you direct your attention. In the whirlwind of contemporary life, it is all too simple to get swept away by the chaos. However, establishing clear priorities is essential to guarantee that your family's time and energy are devoted to what truly matters.

1. **Quality Time:** A fundamental priority for any family must be the investment of quality time spent together. Engagement can manifest through family dinners, game nights, or by dedicating regular one-on-one time with each child.
Consider reserving Sunday evenings for family engagement, during which all members put aside their devices to partake in a collective activity, such as preparing a meal together or enjoying board games.

2. **Education and Personal Growth**: Place a strong emphasis on your children's education and personal development by nurturing a passion for learning, whether through academic pursuits, hobbies, or life experiences.
Example: Should education take precedence, consider dedicating time each day for reading, completing homework, or collectively delving into new subjects as a family. Furthermore, inspire your children to explore passions outside of their academic environment, including music, sports, or the arts.

3. **Health and Well-being:** Prioritise the physical and emotional well-being of your family. This includes a focus on balanced nutrition, consistent physical activity, and the importance of mental well-being.
Example: If health is a priority, engage your children in the planning and preparation of nutritious meals, or create a routine for regular physical activities, such as family walks or bike rides.

4, **Community and Social Connections:** Encourage your children to foster strong relationships within the community, whether through friendships, extended family ties, or engaging in community service.
Example: Should community be a priority, consider engaging in local events,

volunteering as a family, or regularly visiting relatives and acquaintances to strengthen social bonds.

Final Thoughts

Defining values and priorities serves as a fundamental aspect of intentional parenting. It requires thoughtful consideration and unwavering commitment, yet the benefits are significant. Establishing clear values provides a solid foundation for your family, guiding your children's behaviour and supporting their overall development. By focussing on what is genuinely important, you ensure that your family's time and energy are dedicated to fulfilling endeavours. As you navigate your parenting journey, remember that while your values and priorities may shift, the dedication to living with purpose and intention will always be at the core of your family's success.

III

Fostering a Supportive environment for Your Child

A nurturing environment is characterised by a sense of security, affection, and respect for children. This is a domain where individuals can explore the world, learn from their experiences, and develop into confident, skilled persons. As custodians, shaping this environment is a crucial element of our duty. In this segment, we will explore the elements of a supportive environment, approaches to cultivate it within your home, and the lasting influence it can have on your child's development.

Understanding the Importance of a Supportive Atmosphere

Before exploring the establishment of a nurturing environment, it is essential to understand its fundamental importance. The environment in which a child is raised plays a crucial role in shaping their emotional, social, and cognitive development. A supportive atmosphere provides:

1.**Emotional Stability:** Children require a foundation of safety and stability to navigate their environment, face challenges, and develop independence. Emotional stability is fundamental to a child's ability to develop healthy relationships and a positive self-image.

2. **Fostering Growth:** Creating a nurturing environment promotes growth by providing children with opportunities to gain knowledge, participate in

play, and connect with their peers. It functions as a space where they can make mistakes and learn from them, with the guidance and support of their carers.

3. Fostering a Sense of Belonging: Children who view themselves as essential members of their family are more likely to develop a strong sense of self-esteem. The sense of belonging is cultivated through positive interactions and the recognition of their importance within the family structure.

4. Fostering Positive Behavioural Development: When children are raised in a supportive environment, they are more likely to develop healthy behaviours and social skills. They acquire the ability to interact with others in a respectful and understanding way.

5. Fostering Resilience: A supportive environment enables children to develop resilience, the ability to overcome challenges and recover from setbacks. Children who exhibit resilience possess a greater ability to handle stress, adjust to changes, and face life's challenges with confidence.

Essential Elements of a Supportive Environment

Fostering a nurturing environment involves much more than merely addressing your child's fundamental needs. Creating a home environment that fosters love, respect, and growth requires intentional efforts. The essential components of a supportive environment are as follows:

Emotional support

The provision of emotional support establishes the cornerstone of a nurturing environment. Children need to feel loved and accepted for their true selves. This support fosters the development of a secure attachment, essential for their emotional and social growth.

· **Exhibit Unconditional Affection:** Cherish your child for their inherent value, rather than their achievements. Unconditional love guarantees that your child recognises they are valued, regardless of their successes or failures.

· **Attune to Their Needs:** Remain vigilant to your child's emotional cues and respond with care. Recognising their needs for solace, encouragement, or space fosters a sense of acknowledgement and support.

· **Validate Their Emotions:** Acknowledge your child's feelings, even if you do not always agree. Recognising their emotions shows respect for their perspective and assists them in developing skills to navigate their feelings.

• **Provide Comfort and Reassurance:** During periods of stress or uncertainty, extend comfort and reassurance. This may be expressed through physical gestures, such as a hug, or through verbal affirmations aimed at fostering confidence.

Rather than dismissing your child's feelings following a tough day at school, take a moment to sit with them and express, "I can sense your distress." Are you open to discussing the events that transpired? This method effectively communicates your emotional support, irrespective of the situation.

The physical environment

The physical environment of your home is crucial in creating a supportive atmosphere. A nurturing environment that is safe, welcoming, and engaging can greatly enhance a child's development.

• **Safe and Secure Household:** Guarantee that your home is physically secure for your child. This includes securing hazardous areas, anchoring substantial furniture, and ensuring that harmful substances are kept out of reach.
• **Inviting Living Spaces:** Design environments that promote comfort and tranquilly for your child. This may encompass inviting nooks designed for reading, engaging in play, and relaxing.
• **Organized and Clutter-Free:** An orderly and uncluttered environment contributes to reducing stress and anxiety for both you and your child. It also promotes convenient access to essentials and participation in activities without interruptions.
• **Engaging and Intriguing:** Offer a diverse selection of age-appropriate toys, books, and resources that encourage exploration and learning. Regularly rotating toys and materials preserves their charm and keeps engagement high.

Example: Create a cozy reading nook in your child's room featuring a comfortable chair, a small bookshelf, and sufficient lighting for an inviting atmosphere. Inspire your child to dedicate time each day to this space, fostering a passion for reading while providing a tranquil environment for unwinding.

Regular Practices

Children flourish in environments characterised by consistency and predictability. Consistent routines foster a sense of stability and help children understand what to expect in their everyday experiences.

• **Daily Regimens:** Establish consistent routines for morning rituals, meals, playtime, and bedtime. This helps children cultivate a sense of organisation and responsibility.

• **Rituals and Customs:** Create family rituals and traditions that your child can look forward to, such as weekly game nights, holiday celebrations, or bedtime stories.

• **Explicit Expectations:** Clearly articulate your expectations concerning behaviour and responsibilities. The consistent enforcement of rules and expectations enables children to understand boundaries and develop self-discipline.

• **Flexibility Within Structure:** While consistency holds significant importance, embracing flexibility is equally essential. Life is full of surprises, and guiding your child to embrace changes in routine cultivates resilience.

Example: Establish a bedtime routine that incorporates soothing activities such as reading a story, brushing teeth, and saying goodnight. This routine's consistency promotes a seamless transition to sleep for your child, fostering a sense of security through the predictability of nightly expectations.

Effective Communication

Effective and positive communication is essential for fostering a strong and supportive relationship with your child. It involves not just speaking, but also engaging in active listening and understanding.

• **Attentive Listening:** Engage in active listening with your child, providing them with your full attention to ensure they feel recognised and valued. This requires eliminating distractions and focussing intently on their words.

• **Empathy and Insight:** Show understanding by striving to view situations through your child's perspective. Comprehending their thoughts and emotions contributes significantly to building trust and connection.

• **Encouraging Feedback:** Utilise positive reinforcement to inspire and promote desirable behaviour. Recognise and praise your child's efforts and achievements, no matter how small, to enhance their confidence and sense of self-worth.

· Clarity and Serenity in Communication: Articulate your expectations and regulations with clarity and calmness. Avoid employing harsh language or elevating your voice, as such actions may evoke fear and discomfort.

Example: When your child faces frustration while working on homework, rather than immediately stepping in to correct them, pause to hear their concerns. One might say, "I recognise that this issue presents a considerable challenge for you. Let us work together to address it." This method illustrates your support rather than merely concentrating on the final outcome.

Support and Guidance

An environment that fosters growth is one in which children are inspired to explore, embrace challenges, and follow their interests. Your support can foster confidence and ignite a passion for learning.

· Encourage Exploration: Provide your child with opportunities to explore their interests, whether through extracurricular activities, hobbies, or educational trips.

· Recognise Endeavour, Beyond Results: Emphasise the importance of effort rather than solely focusing on outcomes. Honour your child's dedication and perseverance, regardless of the results.

· Encourage Independence: Inspire your child to explore new activities and make choices on their own, while providing support when needed. This promotes the cultivation of independence and enhances problem-solving abilities.

· Be Their Most Enthusiastic Advocate: Show genuine enthusiasm and unwavering support for your child's endeavours, be it a school project, a sports event, or a creative pursuit.

Example: Should your child express a passion for art, provide them with the necessary materials and a dedicated space to unleash their creativity. Visit their art exhibitions or display their artwork in your home to express your appreciation and support for their passion.

Creating Healthy Boundaries

A nurturing environment is characterised by affection and care, yet it also involves the establishment of healthy boundaries. Boundaries provide a framework that helps children understand the parameters of acceptable behaviour.

- **Establishing Clear Regulations:** Implement explicit, age-appropriate guidelines that are consistently enforced. This helps children understand what is expected of them and the consequences of their actions.
- **Encourage Respect:** Teach your child the significance of honouring boundaries—both personal and those of others. This encompasses respecting personal space, safeguarding privacy, and upholding the rights of individuals.
- **Striking a Balance Between Freedom and Accountability:** Allow your child the autonomy to make choices while simultaneously ensuring they are held accountable for their decisions. This promotes an understanding of responsibility and the repercussions of their decisions.
- **Consistency and Impartiality:** It is essential to maintain consistency in the enforcement of boundaries. It is essential to maintain fairness and flexibility, modifying boundaries as your child grows and their needs change.

Example: Implement a guideline requiring that electronic screens be turned off by a specified time each evening. Clarify the importance of this rule in sustaining a healthy sleep regimen. Consistently uphold the rule, yet remain receptive to conversations regarding exceptions, such as a designated movie night.

Behavioural Modelling

Children gain a significant amount of knowledge by observing their parents. Exhibiting positive behaviour emerges as one of the most effective ways to instill in your child the values and practices you desire them to adopt.

- **Exemplify Your Teachings:** Demonstrate the behaviours and principles you wish for your child to adopt. To inspire others to embody kindness, respect, and responsibility, it is essential that your own behaviour reflects these virtues. Children exhibit sharp observational abilities and frequently imitate the behaviours they observe in their parents.
- **Exhibit Empathy and Compassion:** Demonstrate empathy by being attuned to the emotions and needs of others. Demonstrating kindness

to a stranger or exhibiting composure in the face of adversity can be remarkably simple yet profoundly impactful. Your child will understand the importance of empathy by observing you demonstrate it in your daily interactions.

- **Approach Conflict with Composure:** Children keenly observe your responses to stress and disagreement. By addressing challenges with calmness and rational thought, you set an example for others to follow. This involves managing your emotions, communicating clearly, and recognising productive solutions to challenges.
- **Promote Healthy Habits:** Your approach to health and wellness—encompassing dietary choices, physical activity, and self-care—can significantly influence your child's perceptions of their own well-being. Exhibit a balanced lifestyle that emphasises comprehensive well-being.

To foster good manners in your child, consistently employ polite language within the home environment. Consistently use expressions such as "please" and "thank you," and extend respect to others, even in difficult circumstances. Your child will effortlessly incorporate these behaviours into their unique communication style.

Fostering a Growth Mindset

Fostering a growth mindset—the conviction that skills and intelligence can be developed through commitment and hard work—is essential for a child's success and resilience. Fostering this mindset in your child can significantly influence their attitude towards challenges and the learning process.

- **Foster a Love for Learning:** Highlight the excitement of discovery and knowledge acquisition, rather than merely concentrating on grades or results. Encourage your child to ask questions and explore new ideas to foster a sense of curiosity.
- **Recognise Effort, Not Just Achievement:** Praise your child's hard work and determination, regardless of whether the outcomes meet expectations. This underscores the belief that diligence and determination are valuable, regardless of the results.
- **Foster an Understanding of Mistakes:** Help your child recognise that errors are a fundamental part of the learning process. Rather than

fearing failure, encourage them to see it as an opportunity for growth and improvement.

- **Offer Opportunities for Challenge:** Allow your child to engage with challenges that expand their limits. Provide them with support during these challenges, offering guidance and motivation, while avoiding direct intervention to resolve their issues for them.

Example: When your child faces a challenging maths problem, instead of providing the answer, commend their effort and assist them in navigating the steps to uncover the solution. I genuinely appreciate the dedication you are putting into this. Let us consider the actions you can undertake to address the issue at hand. This method emphasises the importance of determination and analytical reasoning.

Encouraging Social Bonds

Social bonds play a crucial role in a child's development. A nurturing environment provides opportunities for your child to build meaningful connections with family, friends, and the wider community.

- **Promote Family Unity:** Dedicate quality time to family, participating in activities that enhance connection and communication. This may involve communal dining, engaging game evenings, or adventurous outings in nature.
- **Foster Friendships:** Support your child in developing friendships by creating opportunities for social engagement. This may occur through play dates, school activities, or community events.
- **Teach Social Etiquette:** Support your child in developing vital social skills, including sharing, teamwork, and conflict resolution. Engaging in role-playing scenarios and contemplating social contexts can aid individuals in effectively managing their interactions with others.
- **Engage Your Child in Community Affairs:** Involvement in community activities, such as volunteering or attending local events, can assist your child in developing a sense of belonging and social responsibility.

Plan a family volunteering day at a nearby charitable organisation or community event. This not only fortifies your family connection but also instills in your child the importance of generosity and being an essential member of a larger community.

Fostering Imagination and Playfulness

Play is a fundamental aspect of childhood, offering opportunities for learning, creativity, and emotional expression. A supportive environment provides abundant opportunities for play and exploration.

- **Encourage Unstructured Play:** Allow your child the freedom to participate in unstructured play, enabling them to tap into their imagination and creativity without the constraints of specific goals or rules. This type of play is essential for cognitive and social growth.
- **Foster Creative Expression:** Inspire engagement in artistic activities like drawing, painting, crafting, or storytelling. These efforts support your child in expressing their emotions, developing problem-solving abilities, and discovering their interests.
- **Limit Screen Time:** Although digital media offers educational opportunities, it is essential to balance screen time with alternative forms of play. Inspire your child to embrace the outdoors, engage in physical pursuits, and connect with their peers.
- **Engage in the Joy:** Involve yourself in your child's play activities when suitable. Engaging in joint play strengthens your connection and allows you to guide their play towards constructive outcomes.

Set up a dedicated arts and crafts station at home, equipped with a variety of materials including paper, markers, glue, and repurposed items. Inspire your child to bring their visions to life, and participate in the experience by creating something of your own. This approach not only fosters creativity but also provides a delightful, collective experience.

The Enduring Benefits of a Supportive Environment

Creating a supportive atmosphere for your child brings significant and lasting advantages. Children nurtured in a supportive, loving, and organised environment are more likely to develop into well-adjusted, resilient, and successful adults. Here are several lasting benefits:

1. **Emotional fortitude:** children who experience security and nurturing are more prepared to face the challenges of life. They foster resilience, allowing

them to recover from setbacks and persist in the midst of challenges.

2. **Positive relationship:** A nurturing environment fosters in children the capacity to develop healthy, constructive relationships. They understand the importance of empathy, communication, and respect, which are essential for building strong relationships with others.

3.**Self-Respect and Assurance:** When children are valued and supported, they develop a strong sense of self-esteem. This assurance enables individuals to chase their ambitions, embrace calculated risks, and trust in their own abilities.

4. **Lifelong Knowledge:** A commitment to lifelong learning, cultivated within a nurturing environment, remains with a child for a lifetime. They transform into curious, motivated individuals who welcome fresh concepts and experiences.

5. **Ethical and Moral Principles:** Children raised in a nurturing environment, rich with clear values, are more likely to cultivate a strong moral compass. They understand the significance of integrity, honesty, and compassion, which steer them in making principled decisions.

6. **Independence and Accountability:** A nurturing environment cultivates children's independence while highlighting the importance of accountability. Individuals acquire the skills to make informed decisions, confront challenges, and assume accountability for their actions.

Final Thoughts

Creating a supportive environment is an ongoing and evolving journey that adjusts in response to your child's growth. It requires a deliberate approach, unwavering consistency, and a deep commitment to your child's well-being. By providing emotional support, establishing clear boundaries, encouraging exploration, and modelling positive behaviour, you lay the foundation for your child's lasting success and happiness.

Keep in mind that no environment is perfect, and challenges will emerge throughout the journey. The essence of success resides in the ability to remain flexible, addressing your child's changing requirements, and consistently fostering a nurturing and supportive atmosphere that enables their growth. By fostering this nurturing environment, you not only assist your child in becoming a confident and capable individual, but also strengthen the familial bond that connects your family, creating a lasting legacy of love and support.

IV
Overcoming Parenting Obstacles

Being a parent is rewarding, but it also comes with its fair share of challenges that test a parent's emotional resilience, patience, and resilience. In this chapter, we will explore common challenges that parents face, find ways to overcome them, and turn them into opportunities for growth for both themselves and their children.

Understanding the Crux of Parenting Obstacles
Difficulties are an inevitable part of being a parent, but it's important to remember that every parent faces them. Difficulties arise from a variety of sources, such as your own expectations, your child's developmental stages, and societal pressures. From managing work and family responsibilities to dealing with behavioural issues and academic demands, these challenges can come in all shapes and sizes.

It is helpful to see these difficulties not as bad encounters but as opportunities for growth and learning. Your approach to these challenges will have a profound effect on your child's development and your relationship with them.

Typical Obstacles Faced by Parents and Strategies for Conquering Them

1. Difficulties with Behaviour

Understanding the Difficulty: Children often struggle with behavioral issues like tantrums, disobedience, and aggression, especially during certain stages of development like early childhood and adolescence. Coping with these behaviours can be frustrating and vexing.

Methods for Overcoming:
• **Be Consistent and Keep Your Cool:** It's important to keep your cool when your child acts out. Anger and frustration are negative emotions that can make things worse. Your child will learn the consequences of their actions more effectively if you are consistent with your disciplinary approach.
• **Get to the Bottom of Things:** A lot of the time, problems with behaviour are signs of deeper issues, like frustration, fear, or a need for attention. Make an effort to identify and resolve the underlying causes of your child's behaviour.
• **Set Clear Boundaries:** Communicate clear rules and expectations for conduct that are suitable for the child's age. It is important that your child understands the consequences of crossing these boundaries.
• **Positive Reinforcement:** Focus on praising good behaviour instead of just punishing bad behaviour; this is known as positive reinforcement. When your child does something good, make sure to praise and reward them. This will encourage them to keep doing it.

For example, instead of giving in or reacting harshly when your child throws a tantrum over a denied toy at the store, try explaining calmly why the toy is not available and suggesting a way they can earn it, like by being good. Eventually, they'll realise that throwing a tantrum won't get them anywhere and will start controlling their emotions better.

Keeping a Healthy Work-Life Balance

Realising the Obstacle: Many parents struggle to balance their work responsibilities with the needs of their family. Worry, shame, and feelings of inadequate performance in either function may ensue from this.

Methods for Conquering:
• **Prioritise and delegate:** Give your full attention to the things that are most important to you, whether they are work-related or personal. Whether at home or at the office, delegate tasks when possible.

• **Define Limits:** Make sure there is a clear separation between your work time and your family time. Establishing and strictly sticking to regular work and family schedules might be one way to achieve this goal.

• **Quality Over Quantity:** It's more important to focus on the quality of your time with your child than the amount of time you spend with them. Spend the time you have together doing things that matter, paying attention fully, and making memories that will last a lifetime.

• **Self-Care:** Taking care of yourself is crucial if you want to be a good parent and worker. Make sure you give yourself time to do things you enjoy, whether that's exercising, engaging in a hobby, or just relaxing.

Example set up a specific work area and time each day if you are going to be working from home. Schedule times when you can spend quality time with your child, like reading a book or going for a short walk, and make sure they know these limits.

Limiting Computer Use

The Problem: In this technological age, it can be very difficult to limit your child's screen time. Even though screens are super important for learning and entertainment, using them too much can make you sluggish, have trouble sleeping, and even isolate yourself from others.

Methods for Conquering:

Limit your child's screen time in a way that is appropriate for their age. Limiting the kinds of content they can access or setting specific times for screen usage (like after homework) are two ways to achieve this goal.

• **Encourage Other Activities:** Give kids things to do besides staring at screens, like reading, playing outside, or creating art. As an alternative to mindless screen time, you should encourage your child to participate in these activities.

• **Be a Good Example:** Display good screen habits yourself. You can encourage your child to maintain a healthy screen-to-life balance by setting a good example yourself.

• **Monitor Content:** Keep yourself updated on what your child is seeing and doing online by monitoring the content they are engaging with. Make sure it's age-appropriate and talk to them about anything that worries them.

Example: Establish a rule that your child must complete their homework and participate in at least 30 minutes of physical activity before using screens, for example, if they tend to spend too much time on their tablet. As a result, there is less chance of spending too much time in front of screens and a more balanced lifestyle.

Pressure from School

The Pressure to Make Sure Your Child Does Well in School is Real for Many Parents. Parental expectations, peer pressure, or high hopes for their child's future achievements might all contribute to this kind of pressure. But, parents and children alike can experience stress and burnout as a result of an unhealthy obsession with schoolwork.

Methods for Conquering:

• **Prioritise Education Above All Elements:** Highlight the importance of a love of learning and a thirst for knowledge above superficial academic success. Your child is more likely to have meaningful academic experiences if you encourage them to pursue interests outside of school.

• **Give Help Without Pressuring:** If you want your child to do well in school, you should give them what they need to succeed, but you shouldn't force them to do anything. Assure them that it's okay to struggle and that making an attempt is more important than striving for perfection.

• **Encourage a Well-Rounded Life:** Help your child strike a balance between school, extracurriculars, and downtime to promote a well-rounded life. Their general health depends on this equilibrium.

• **Maintain Communication with Educators:** Communicate with your child's teachers on a regular basis to learn about their progress and pinpoint any areas where they might need extra help. You can provide your child with a more well-rounded education by working together with teachers.

Example: Instead of concentrating only on grades, you and your child can work together to find fun and interesting ways to practise maths, like using educational games or finding real-world applications. This can help if your child is having trouble with maths. Learning becomes more enjoyable and less stressful with this approach.

Family Conflict

The Difficulty: Sibling rivalry is a common problem in households where there are many children. It can cause strife in the family dynamic by surfacing as rivalry, jealousy, or frequent arguments.

Methods for Conquering:

• **Recognize Each Child's Uniqueness:** Don't compare your kids to each other; instead, focus on how unique they are. Recognise and honour their unique qualities and achievements.

• **Foster Teamwork and Collaboration Rather Than Competitiveness:** Advocate for activities that bring siblings together in a cooperative spirit. Emphasise the value of a united front and mutual support.

Ensure Equity: Equal distribution of rules and responsibilities is something you should strive for as a parent. This aids in avoiding sentiments of partiality and animosity.

Mediate Disputes: Assist your children in seeing things from each other's points of view and remain calm as you mediate disagreements. Instruct them on healthy ways to communicate their feelings and how to resolve conflicts.

Example If your kids are fighting over a toy, for instance, rather than picking a side, you should encourage them to work together to find a solution. You might pose the question, "How can we fix this problem such that everyone is happy?" This method promotes teamwork and teaches people to resolve conflicts.

Handling Outside Factors

The Problem: Cultural norms, media portrayals, and friends all have a greater impact on children as they grow up. Problems and challenges to your parenting principles may arise as a result of these influences.

Methods for Conquering:

• **Tell Your Child What's Important:** Make sure your child knows what your family's fundamental values are and why they're important. This helps clarify your point of view and the thinking behind your expectations.

· **Foster Critical Thinking:** Teach your child that when confronted with outside influences, such as media messages or peer pressure, it is important to think critically. Make sure they ask questions and think about how their choices will affect others.

· **Monitor External Influences:** Keep an eye on your child's friends and how much time they spend in front of the TV. Discuss these influences with your loved ones and figure out whether they fit in with or go against your family's principles.

· **Keep Involved:** Never let go of your child's side, no matter how much independence they develop. You can help them through tough times and strengthen your bond with them if you stay involved.

For instance, if your child is influenced by a friend to act in an undesirable way, it's important to have a candid conversation about it. Say something like, "I've noticed that you've been spending a lot of time with this friend. Let's talk about how their decisions mesh with our family's principles.This method stresses the significance of maintaining family values and promotes self-reflection.

How To Reframe Challenges As Opportunities:
Parenting isn't always easy, but it's also full of learning experiences, for you and your child. Here's a way to see obstacles in a positive light:

1. **Growth Through Adversity:** you can learn resilience, problem-solving, and persistence through adversity. Your ability to handle adversity with grace and optimism will be an example to your child.

2. **Learning Together:** you can learn a lot as a family by taking on challenges together. Tackling challenges as a family strengthens bonds, whether it's navigating a developmental phase or dealing with outside influences.

3. **Cultivating Empathy and Understanding:** Responding to difficulties with empathy and understanding teaches your child the value of taking into account the feelings and perspectives of others. This encourages the development of empathy and emotional intelligence.

4. **Strengthening Bonds:** Conquering obstacles side by side can strengthen the bond you share with your child. Building trust and a stronger bond occurs when they see you as someone they can turn to for advice and encouragement.

5. **Teaching Your Child Important Life Skills:** One of the most difficult parts

of being a parent is teaching your child important life skills like how to deal with stress, how to organise their time well, and how to think critically. With these abilities, they will be able to handle the challenges that life throws at them.

Welcome to the Adventure of Parenting!
There will be many ups and downs on the journey of parenthood. With a growth mindset, understanding, and patience, you can overcome these obstacles and turn them into chances for your child and yourself to thrive. Being an engaged and purposeful parent is more important than striving for perfection. Accept and overcome obstacles as they come; in doing so, you will strengthen your family bond while also learning and growing.

Always remember that you have company on your parenting journey. You can make a huge difference by reaching out for support, whether it's from your partner, family, friends, or professionals. Every parent faces challenges. As a couple, you can handle all the challenges of parenting and provide your child with a loving home where they can thrive.

V
The Power of Positive Reinforcement in Parenting

Using positive reinforcement is a powerful way to influence your child's behaviour, attitude, and self-esteem. In this chapter, we're going to dive into positive reinforcement. We'll look at what it's all about, its psychological roots, the benefits it brings, and how you can apply it in real life. Let us chat about how we can use it effectively to encourage positive behaviour and build a strong, healthy relationship between parents and kids.

Getting a grip on positive reinforcement

Positive reinforcement is all about encouraging good behaviours by giving rewards or praise once those behaviours happen. This idea comes from behavioural psychology, especially the work of B.F. Skinner, who showed that when behaviours lead to positive results, people are more likely to do them again.

There are so many ways positive reinforcement can show up, like:
· **Verbal Acclaim:** It is all about acknowledging and appreciating your child's hard work and achievements.
· **Physical Demonstrations of Affection:** You can show your appreciation with warm embraces, high-fives, or a gentle tap on the back when someone does something great.
· **Material Rewards:** How about offering some small incentives like stickers,

toys, or maybe even a bit of extra playtime? That could be fun!
· **Privileges:** Allowing your child to join in on a favourite activity or giving them a bit more freedom because they have been behaving well.

Positive reinforcement is all about encouraging the behaviours you want to see more of, like compassion, accountability, persistence, and collaboration. It's a great way to build a supportive environment!

Positive reinforcement can really make a difference in how we learn and grow. It encourages good behaviour and boosts confidence, making it a powerful tool for motivation. By focussing on the positives, we can create a more supportive environment for ourselves and others.

When used the right way, positive reinforcement can bring a lot of benefits for both kids and parents:

1. **Boosting Self-Esteem and Confidence:** Positive reinforcement helps kids build a sense of competence. When their efforts are recognised and valued, they start to believe in themselves more, which boosts their self-esteem.
2. **Promoting Good Behaviour:** When parents highlight and encourage positive actions, it helps inspire their kids to do the same. This helps create good habits and reduces the need for discipline.
3. **Strengthening the Connection Between Parents and Kids:** Using positive reinforcement helps build a loving and supportive bond between parents and their kids. Kids who feel valued and recognised tend to have a stronger bond with their parents.
4. **Fostering Long-Term Development:** With time, kids really start to take in the values and behaviours that are encouraged around them. It is great to see them learning to act responsibly, showing empathy, and working hard, even when there are not any rewards coming their way.
5. **Mitigating Negative Behaviours:** You know, while positive reinforcement is all about boosting the good stuff, it also helps to reduce those not-so-great behaviours without even trying too hard. When kids get praise for good behaviour, they are less likely to act out for attention in negative ways.

Understanding the Psychology of Positive Reinforcement
Positive reinforcement comes from the idea of operant conditioning, which is a theory in behavioural psychology that explains how our actions are

shaped by the outcomes they produce. There are four main types of reinforcement:

1. Positive Reinforcement: This means adding something nice to encourage a behaviour to happen again, like praising a child for cleaning their room.
2. Negative Reinforcement: Negative reinforcement involves removing something unpleasant to encourage a certain behaviour. For example, if a child finishes their homework on time, they might be allowed to skip their chores.
3. Positive Punishment: This involves adding something unpleasant to reduce the likelihood of a behaviour, like scolding a child for being rude.
4. Negative Punishment: This involves taking away something enjoyable to reduce a behaviour, like taking away screen time when there is misbehaviour.

When it comes to parenting, using positive reinforcement is really the best way to go. It helps build cooperation and supports personal growth without needing to resort to fear or punishment.

Here are some practical ways to use positive reinforcement.

1. Offer Clear and Detailed Compliments

You know saying something like "Good job!" can feel a bit vague. It's way more helpful to give specific feedback instead. Kids really need to understand what they did well to feel motivated to do it again.

Here's how you can go about implementing it:
• **Identify the Behaviour:** Rather than giving a general compliment, focus on the specific action that deserves recognition from your child. For example, "I really admire how generous you are in sharing your toys with your friend."
• **Recognize the Effort:** It is important to appreciate not just the results, but also the hard work that went into achieving them. This helps your child understand that hard work is just as important as achieving success. Hey, I just wanted to say that you really showed great effort in your math assignment today. That is amazing!
Instead of just saying, "Thanks for helping," you could say, "I really appreciate how you took the time to organise your toys so well." Your sense of responsibility is really impressive!

2. Make sure to use immediate reinforcement.

Reinforcement works best when it is given right after the behaviour happens. Getting quick feedback helps kids connect their actions with a positive reaction.

Here's how you can go about implementing it:

• **Commend in the Moment:** Try to give praise or rewards right away, don't hold back. Hey, if your kid cleans up their room, make sure to give them a shout-out for their hard work right away.

• **Stay Committed:** Make sure to always follow through with positive reinforcement. When you promise a reward for a certain behaviour, make sure to give it right after the behaviour happens.

When your child finishes their homework on their own, make sure to let them know how proud you are by saying something like, "I'm really proud of you for doing your homework all by yourself!"

3. Balance Tangible Rewards with Intrinsic Motivation

Getting the Strategy Right: Sure, tangible rewards like toys or treats can be great motivators, but it is really important to balance those with intrinsic motivation—the satisfaction that comes from doing a task well.

Here's how you can go about implementing it:

• **Focus on Praise Instead of Rewards:** Make sure to highlight verbal encouragement and emotional backing rather than relying on material incentives. This helps your child feel proud of their own actions instead of relying on outside rewards.

• **Introduce Deferred Gratification:** Help your child understand the importance of working towards long-term goals. Instead of giving small rewards for little wins, why not offer bigger rewards for sticking with it over the long haul?

If your child helps out with chores regularly during the week, consider treating them to a fun outing as a reward. Just make sure to highlight that their daily efforts are recognised with some kind words throughout the journey.

4. Embrace challenges as opportunities for growth.

Positive reinforcement can really help kids tackle challenges with a mindset focused on growth. It encourages them to see difficulties as chances to learn instead of obstacles.

Here's how you can go about implementing it:

· **Celebrate Problem-Solving Efforts**: When your child takes on a challenging task, praise their method instead of just the results. Hey, you really kept your cool and tackled that puzzle with some serious thought, even when things got tough. That's impressive! That is really impressive!

· **Celebrate Progress**: It is important to acknowledge your child's progress, even if they are not quite mastering a skill yet. This highlights how important it is to keep improving all the time.

For instance, if your child is getting the hang of riding a bicycle but faces some bumps along the way, you might say, "I really admire how you keep going, even when things get tough." Every time you get up, you are getting closer to riding on your own!

5. Encourage Self-Reflection As your child grows, encourage them to reflect on their actions and the praise they get. This practice really helps you become more self-aware and encourages you to embrace positive behaviours.

Here are the guidelines for execution:

· **Ask Thoughtful Questions**: After giving praise, help your child think about their behaviour. For example, you might ask, "What do you think about your choice to share your toys today?" This helps create a link between good feelings and doing the right thing.

· **Help with Goal Setting**: Get your child involved in setting personal goals and talk about the steps they can take to achieve them. Try using positive reinforcement to encourage them as they work towards their goals.

Illustration: If your child sets a goal to complete a school project ahead of schedule, you might say, "What strategies can you think of to help you meet the deadline?" What can I do to help you out? Make sure to recognise their hard work as they hit those small milestones along the way.

Typical Mistakes and Ways to Avoid Them

Even though positive reinforcement works really well, there are some common mistakes you should watch out for:

1. **Counting on Material Rewards**: Getting rewards for every good thing you do can actually make you less motivated if those rewards stop coming. To tackle this, focus on the importance of intrinsic rewards like praise and

building emotional connections.

2. Inconsistent Application of Reinforcement: Inconsistent application of reinforcement can really confuse kids. Going back and forth between praising a behaviour one day and ignoring it the next can really create confusion about what's expected. Sticking to a consistent approach in reinforcement is really important.

3. Accidental Reinforcement of Negative Behaviour: Just be careful not to accidentally encourage any bad behaviour. You know, when a child gets rewarded or gets attention after throwing a tantrum, it can actually encourage them to keep acting that way to get what they want. Make sure that any reinforcement you give focuses only on the positive things people do.

4. Not Being Specific: Vague or general praise might not have the effect you are hoping for. Kids really benefit from clear feedback on what they did well, so they can keep doing it in the future.

Using Positive Reinforcement with Different Age Groups

It is interesting how positive reinforcement can change depending on how old the child is and where they are in their development. Adjust your strategy like this:

1. Toddlers (Ages 1-3): At this stage, simple rewards like stickers, praise, and affection really work well. Hey, you know, toddlers really thrive when they get immediate praise for things like sharing, following rules, and being polite. It makes a big difference!

2. Preschoolers (Ages 3-5): Preschoolers, those little ones aged 3 to 5, are starting to understand more complex ways of receiving praise and rewards. It's a great idea to encourage social behaviours such as cooperation and empathy by giving specific praise and small rewards. It really helps to reinforce those positive actions!

3. School-Age Children (Ages 6-12): School-age kids, between 6 and 12, really thrive with some kind of structured reinforcement, like charts or point systems. It helps keep them motivated and engaged! It is important to recognise your academic achievements, social skills, and the responsibilities you handle, like doing chores.

4. Teens (Ages 13+): For teens aged 13 and up, it is really important to focus on positive reinforcement that highlights their independence and responsibility. It is great to recognise sound decision-making, self-discipline, and perseverance! You might consider giving some verbal praise and maybe even some privileges like an extended curfew or extra screen time as a reward.

Creating a Positive Reinforcement Framework for Lasting Success

Using positive reinforcement is such an important way to help kids grow into confident, responsible, and emotionally strong people. When parents recognise and encourage good behaviours, they can help their kids develop lasting positive habits, strengthen their relationship, and boost their sense of accomplishment and self-worth.

To build a strong positive reinforcement system, it is important for parents to stay consistent, be specific, and keep in mind where their child is in their development. When you encourage good behaviour with praise, love, and sometimes little rewards, kids start to really understand and embrace those behaviours. This helps them develop a sense of motivation from within instead of just depending on outside rewards.

As kids grow up, the way we encourage them shifts from giving out physical rewards to helping them reflect on themselves, stick with things, and understand their feelings better. As kids grow from little ones to teenagers, there are so many chances for parents to help them learn, grow, and thrive by using positive reinforcement.

At the end of the day, using positive reinforcement goes beyond just managing behaviour in the moment. It is really about helping kids build the skills, confidence, and emotional strength they need for success throughout their lives. When done right, positive reinforcement can really create lasting and meaningful changes. It sets the stage for fulfilling relationships, personal growth, and achievements that stick with you.

When parents focus on creating a positive and nurturing environment, they really set their kids up to grow into empathetic, responsible, and confident people. Positive reinforcement is not just a tactic; it is a way of life that helps kids reach their full potential now and down the road.

VI
Setting Boundaries with Love and Understanding

Establishing boundaries for children are one of the most crucial and, at times, challenging elements of parenting. Establishing boundaries is essential for children's development, as they define acceptable behaviour, impart values, and cultivate a sense of security. However if boundaries are not communicated with warmth and understanding they may be perceived as harsh or authoritarian.

This chapter explores the ways in which parents can establish healthy and constructive boundaries that foster growth, respect, and trust, all while maintaining a nurturing and supportive relationship with their children. We will explore the importance of boundaries for both children and parents, the role of consistency, and how to adapt boundaries as children grow and develop.

The Importance of Boundaries in Parenting

Boundaries serve multiple crucial roles in a child's development:

1. Establishing Structure and Stability: Boundaries play a crucial role in creating routines and expectations that provide children with a sense of order and predictability. This stability offers children a profound sense of security, clarifying expectations and allowing them to anticipate their environment with confidence.

2. Fostering Responsibility and Accountability: Boundaries help children understand the importance of responsibility and the consequences of their actions. Through the acknowledgement of the boundaries and repercussions of their actions, children cultivate self-discipline and a sense of accountability.

3. Nurturing Emotional and Social Development: Establishing boundaries is essential for guiding children in navigating social interactions and relationships. They cultivate an understanding of the importance of respecting others' boundaries, opinions, and emotions, and consequently, they expect to receive the same level of respect in return.

4. Encouraging Independence: While boundaries establish limits, they simultaneously foster independence by allowing children the freedom to make choices within a secure framework. Defining clear boundaries enables children to engage in exploration, make informed decisions, and tackle problems while ensuring a secure environment.

5. Fostering Trust: When boundaries are set with care and mutual understanding, they strengthen the trust between parent and child. Children come to understand that boundaries exist for their protection, while parents illustrate their appreciation for their child's emotions and viewpoints.

Establishing Boundaries with Compassion and Understanding

Boundaries ought not to be seen as punitive measures; rather, they should be regarded as compassionate frameworks that aid children in navigating their environment. To effectively communicate boundaries, parents should blend firmness with empathy.

1. Elucidate the Justification for the Boundaries

Children are more inclined to honour boundaries when they grasp the reasoning behind them. Rather than framing rules as mere impositions, clarify the rationale behind specific behaviours being deemed unacceptable and illustrate how these boundaries are designed to safeguard their safety, well-being, and respectfulness.

Strategies for Implementation:

• **Provide Explanations Suitable for the Age Group**: Adjust your explanation to match your child's understanding. Simple explanations are the most effective approach for younger children. For example, "We avoid running in the street due to the dangers it presents." For older children, it is beneficial to offer additional context, such as exploring the significance of respecting the time and belongings of others.

• Establish a Link Between Boundaries and Their Real-World Implications: Guide your child in understanding the effects of their actions on both themselves and those around them. For instance, "Failing to submit your homework punctually results in a sense of urgency and robs you of the opportunity to unwind in the evening."

Illustration: When establishing a boundary concerning screen time, you might articulate, "We are implementing a limit on screen time because excessive television viewing can hinder attention to other important activities, such as academic responsibilities and outdoor play."

2. Maintain Consistency with Boundaries

The lack of consistency in setting and upholding boundaries can confuse children and erode their sense of security. Consistency enables children to understand the rules and the repercussions of their behaviours.

Strategies for Implementation:

• Follow the Established Guidelines: Once a boundary is established, it is essential to respect it. When bedtime is set for 8 PM, it is essential to uphold this schedule consistently. In instances where the boundary is occasionally relaxed, it is important to offer a clear explanation to avoid any potential confusion.

• Ensure Alignment Between Both Parents: Consistency among carers is essential. When one parent establishes a boundary while the other does not, children may find themselves confused or may try to test those limits.

Illustration: When you establish a boundary regarding mealtime behaviour, such as "We remain seated at the table until everyone has finished eating," it is crucial to enforce that rule consistently, even in the face of your child's resistance.

3. Exhibit Adaptability When Required

While consistency holds significant importance, it is equally essential to recognise circumstances that demand adaptability. Life often brings unexpected challenges, and a strict adherence to boundaries can occasionally result in unwarranted frustration. Flexibility teaches children that rules can be modified in response to changing circumstances.

Strategies for Implementation:

• Assess the Circumstances: When a boundary is breached as a result of an unforeseen event or the emotional state of a child, it is prudent to take a moment to reflect on whether the rigid enforcement of that boundary is genuinely required at that particular time.

· **Adjust Boundaries with Development:** As your child matures, it is essential to evolve boundaries to align with their growing sense of responsibility and independence. For example, when a child exhibits proficient time management skills, it may be appropriate to contemplate extending curfew hours or adjusting screen time limitations.

For instance, if your child appears particularly tired one evening, you might consider modifying the bedtime routine by allowing them to go to bed 15 minutes earlier and selecting a shorter bedtime story.

4. Employ positive reinforcement alongside established boundaries

The integration of positive reinforcement with established boundaries fosters an environment in which children not only respect limits but also feel recognised and rewarded for their commendable behaviour. This method effectively harmonises discipline with motivation.

Strategies for Implementation:

· **Recognise Positive Behaviour:** When your child follows the set boundaries, provide verbal praise and positive reinforcement. Acknowledge their contributions and convey appreciation for their collaboration.

· **Provide Positive Incentives:** To encourage consistent adherence to boundaries, consider offering additional privileges or rewards, such as extended playtime or the chance to select a family activity.

Illustrative Example: If your child consistently completes their homework before dinner (a boundary you have set), you might express your appreciation by saying, "I commend your responsible approach to homework."Would you be interested in participating in a delightful activity together this coming weekend?"

5. Engage Your Child in the Process of Establishing Boundaries

When children are involved in setting boundaries, they are more likely to respect and adhere to them. Involving them in discussions regarding rules cultivates a sense of ownership and responsibility.

Steps for Implementation:

· **Encourage Their Participation:** Depending on your child's age, invite them to share their thoughts on particular boundaries, such as bedtime, household chores, or screen time. Empower them to participate in the decision-making process, while guaranteeing that the ultimate decisions are logical and implementable.

• **Engage in a Dialogue about Consequences:** When establishing boundaries, initiate conversations regarding the implications of violating them. Help your child understand that consequences are not forms of punishment, but rather the natural results of their decisions.

For instance, when setting a boundary concerning the completion of chores, you might ask, "What consequences do you believe would be suitable if the chores remain unfinished by the end of the day?"This fosters a meaningful conversation in which your child feels acknowledged and valued.

Adjusting Boundaries as Children Develop

As children progress through different stages of development, their needs and abilities change, requiring appropriate modifications to the limits established for them. Understanding when to adjust or soften boundaries is essential for fostering their development.

1. **Young Children (Ages 1-3):** Boundaries for young children must be clear, direct, and promptly enforced. Highlight the importance of safety and essential social standards. For example, "We avoid striking others as it causes pain" or "We join hands when crossing the street."

2. **Early Childhood (Ages 3-5):** As children cultivate their social awareness, it is essential that boundaries incorporate social skills such as sharing and taking turns. Regulations ought to be straightforward while accommodating more comprehensive clarifications. Sharing your toys with your playmate is essential for fostering mutual enjoyment.

3. **School-Age Children (Ages 6-12):** During this developmental phase, children start to understand more complex boundaries and the reasoning that underpins them. Encourage autonomy while setting clear expectations for academic responsibilities, household chores, and behaviour. For example, "Finishing your homework prior to enjoying television is essential."

4. **Teenagers (Ages 13+):** Adolescence signifies an increased desire for independence, and the boundaries established should correspond to this developmental shift. Implement regulations that provide greater autonomy while maintaining safety and respect. Curfews, for example, may be

adjusted with consideration for trust and accountability.

The Importance of Outcomes

The role of consequences is crucial in establishing boundaries. When boundaries are crossed, it is essential that the resulting consequences are reasonable, fair, and clearly articulated.

1. Natural Consequences: Permitting natural consequences to occur (when safe) helps children understand the implications of their actions. For example, when a child neglects to bring their homework, they might face repercussions at school.

2. Logical Consequences: The logical consequences must be directly associated with the behaviour demonstrated. For instance, should a child decline to organise their toys, they may lose the opportunity to engage with them the next day.

3. Consistent yet Compassionate: In the process of enforcing consequences, it is essential to uphold consistency while also embodying compassion. Explain to your child that the consequence arises from their choices, rather than being a punishment imposed by you.

Defining Boundaries as Expressions of Care

Setting boundaries with compassion is one of the most precious gifts you can offer your child. Boundaries provide a foundation of security, accountability, and respect, essential for personal growth and the cultivation of healthy relationships. When combined with empathy, positive reinforcement, and steadfast consistency, boundaries support children in developing into confident, disciplined, and emotionally mature individuals. As a parent, it is essential to understand that boundaries are not merely a means of exerting control; rather, they serve to establish a secure and nurturing environment in which your child can learn, grow, and thrive. When boundaries are established with love, empathy, and mutual respect, they help children understand their own limitations, foster self-discipline, and promote respect for others.

Moreover, boundaries provide children with the opportunity to explore their environment, knowing they have a dependable structure to guide them. Children gain a sense of empowerment in decision-making when they recognise that their parents are present to support them in moments of uncertainty or when they need help grasping the implications of their choices. The fostering of responsibility and independence equips children with vital life skills that they will carry into their adult lives.

Important Takeaways for Setting Boundaries with Care:

1. Boundaries create a sense of safety and consistency. They help kids know what's expected of them and set up a stable environment where they can really flourish.

2. Find the Balance Between Firmness and Empathy: It is really important to be strong but also kind when you are setting boundaries. Kids are more likely to respect boundaries when they understand why those boundaries exist and feel that their feelings and opinions matter.

3. Consistency is Key: Keeping boundaries steady helps kids understand the importance of rules and clears up any confusion about them being random. It really helps build their trust and respect for their parents.

4. Adjust Boundaries with Development: As kids grow and mature, it is important to tweak those boundaries to match their increasing sense of responsibility. Being flexible and keeping the lines of communication open are really important in this process.

5. Use Positive Reinforcement: Recognise good behaviour with praise and support to create a positive link with respecting boundaries. This helps kids really get the hang of good behaviour and feel proud of what they accomplish.

6. Teach Responsibility with Consequences: Using logical and natural consequences helps kids understand what happens as a result of their actions. It is important that these consequences are fair, connected to the behaviour, and applied with understanding.

At the end of the day, setting boundaries with love and understanding is all about helping your child grow into a confident, responsible, and emotionally smart person. When we see boundaries as expressions of love and care, they turn into powerful ways to help kids grow up well, ready to handle life's challenges with empathy, integrity, and a solid sense of who they are.

Creating a space where expectations are clear, respect is mutual, and support is consistent helps your child build the emotional and behavioural skills they need to thrive, not just in their childhood, but for their whole life. Setting boundaries with care and love can really help your child grow into a well-rounded, resilient, and empathetic person, ready to take on the world with confidence and integrity.

Important Takeaways for Setting Boundaries with Care:

1. Boundaries Foster Safety and Consistency: Boundaries create a safe and consistent space for kids. They help children understand what is expected of them and provide a reliable environment where they can really flourish.

2. Find the Balance Between Firmness and Empathy: It is important to be strong but also kind when you are setting boundaries. Kids are more likely to respect boundaries when they understand why those boundaries exist and feel that their feelings and opinions matter.

3. Consistency is Key: Keeping boundaries consistent helps kids understand the importance of rules and clears up any confusion about them being random. It really helps build their trust and respect for their parents.

4. Adjust Boundaries with Development: As kids grow and mature, it is important to tweak boundaries to match their increasing sense of responsibility. Being flexible and keeping the lines of communication open are really important in this process.

5. Use Positive Reinforcement: Recognise good behaviour with praise and support to create a positive link with respecting boundaries. This helps kids really get the hang of good behaviour and feel proud of what they accomplish.

6. Teach Responsibility with Consequences: Logical and natural consequences help kids understand what happens as a result of their actions. It is important that these consequences are fair, connected to the behaviour, and applied with understanding.

At the end of the day, setting boundaries with care and understanding is all about helping your child grow into a confident, responsible, and emotionally savvy person. When we see boundaries as expressions of love and care, they turn into powerful ways to help kids grow up well-adjusted, ready to handle life's challenges with empathy, integrity, and a solid sense of who they are.

When you create a space where expectations are clear, respect is mutual, and support is consistent, you are giving your child the emotional and behavioural tools they need to thrive, not just as kids, but for their whole lives. Setting boundaries with care and love can really help your child grow into a well-rounded, resilient, and empathetic person, ready to take on the world with confidence and integrity.

VII
Navigating Challenging Dialogues with Your Offspring

As kids grow up and change, parents often find themselves in some pretty complex talks. These conversations might cover topics like feeling intimidated, dealing with loss, facing societal pressures, going through physical changes, or mistakes they have made. Many parents find it challenging to talk about these sensitive topics in a way that helps their kids understand and feel confident. The goal of these talks is not just to share information; it is about creating a genuine and open conversation that lasts for your child's whole life.

In this chapter, we'll explore some strategies for tackling tough conversations with kids. We'll share examples and insights to help make these talks more productive and meaningful. We will also chat about why emotional intelligence, really listening, and creating a safe space for open communication are so important.

Why Complex Conversations Matter?

Exploring tough topics helps kids build emotional strength, think critically, and solve problems effectively. When parents talk openly about tough issues, kids understand that it is okay to have difficult feelings or face dilemmas, and they become more confident in tackling challenges on their own. Also, these chats help build trust between parents and kids, creating a safe space that makes it easier for children to open up to their parents when they face other challenges down the road.

Key Principles for Handling Tough Talks
1. **Be Candid, yet Tailored to the Child's Maturity:** Be honest but adjust your approach based on the child's level of understanding. Kids usually pick up on when something feels off, so it is really important to be honest with them. It is really important to adjust how you handle things based on where your child is in their development. Giving a child too much information or complicated details can really confuse or overwhelm them. On the flip side, being unclear can cause misunderstandings or increase anxiety.
Illustration: When a grandparent passes away, a young child might not really understand what death means. Rather than using phrases like "Grandpa went to rest" (which could make someone anxious about sleep), you might say, "Grandpa's physical body stopped working, and he will not be with us anymore."

2. **Create a Safe and Open Environment:** Kids really need to feel safe and recognised when they're exploring tough subjects. A calm and comforting atmosphere allows them to share their feelings without the fear of being judged or punished. The goal is to help them feel comfortable sharing their thoughts and feelings, no matter how complicated or confusing they might seem.
Implementation Strategy:
• Choose a calm and private place for important discussions.
• Stay calm and open-minded, letting your child know that their feelings are completely okay.
• Let your child know that it is totally okay to ask questions, and you will do your best to answer them.

3. **Listen More Than You Speak:** Pay attention to others more than you talk.Being a good listener is super important when it comes to handling tough talks. Sometimes, parents think they need to jump in with answers or advice, but what kids really want is just someone to listen. When we listen without jumping in, it gives kids the chance to really think through their feelings and ideas. It shows that their feelings matter and that you value their perspective.

Implementation strategy:

· Ask open-ended questions to encourage your child to express themselves. So, what was going through your mind when that happened? So what do you think about what happened?

· Summarize what you hear by rephrasing it. It sounds like you are really frustrated about what happened at school.

· Do not rush to provide solutions or downplay your child's feelings. Let them know you are there for them, even if everything is not perfect.

4. Recognise and Affirm Their feelings: It is important for kids to understand that it is okay to feel upset, angry, scared, or confused sometimes. Recognising their feelings helps them feel like someone gets them and is there for them. It is really important to acknowledge how they feel, even if you do not agree with their perspective, to build trust.

Illustration: If your child shares that they are feeling anxious about something, try not to brush off their fear by saying, "There is nothing to be afraid of."Try saying, "I understand why you are feeling scared." It is totally okay to feel that way. Let us talk about it and see how we can help ease your worries.

5. Stay calm and take your time: Talking about tough topics can really stir up strong feelings for both kids and parents. It is really important for parents to stay calm, even when things get tough or emotions run high. Kids often pick up on how their parents react emotionally, so staying calm helps them feel more secure.

Implementation strategy

Take a deep breath and get your feelings in check before diving into a tough chat. If you are feeling a bit off or anxious, it might be a good idea to hold off on the conversation until you're feeling more centered. If your child starts to feel upset or on edge, give them some room to express how they are feeling without making things worse.

Approaches for Various Age Groups

The way you handle tough talks will change based on how old your child is and where they are in their development. Check out these tips for chatting with kids of various ages:

1. For Little Ones (Ages 3-7)

• **Use Simple Language:** Little kids need clear and simple explanations for complex ideas. Use straightforward language to help them understand without making it too complicated.

• **Emphasize Feelings:** At this point, kids are starting to notice and understand their feelings. Focus on helping them recognise and work through their feelings instead of getting into too much detail.

• **Use Stories or Comparisons:** Younger kids usually connect well with stories or comparisons that relate to their own experiences.

For instance, if you are explaining why parents sometimes see things differently, you might say, "Mommy and Daddy don't always agree, just like you and your friend might have different favourite toys." But hey, we still care about one another and we will figure it out together.

2, For kids in the 8 to 12 age range

• **Encourage Questions:** Kids in this age group are super curious and might ask more detailed questions about tough topics. Invite them to ask questions and be ready to give honest, age-appropriate answers.

• **Help with Problem-Solving:** Kids in school are starting to develop their problem-solving skills, so it is great to guide them in thinking about solutions or ways to cope.

• **Offer Comfort:** Kids during this stage might worry about how tough situations will affect them personally. Let them know you are there for them and that things will get better.

For instance, if your child is dealing with bullying, you might say, "I really admire your bravery in sharing this with me." How about we chat about ways to keep you safe?

3. For Teenagers (Ages 13+)

• **Respect Their Autonomy:** Teenagers often want to spread their wings and might not be ready to open up about their feelings right away. Give them the space they need, but let them know you're here whenever they feel ready to chat.

• **Be a Trusted Advisor, Not Just a Parent:** Teens might push back against lectures, but they usually respond more positively to guidance when they feel respected. When tackling tough conversations, try to be empathetic and act like a supportive mentor instead of just being the one in charge.

• **Recognise the Complexity:** Teenagers can understand more complicated issues, so be ready to explore the details of tough subjects. They might have mixed feelings or different opinions, so it is important to create a comfortable space for them to explore those thoughts.

For instance, if your teenager is dealing with peer pressure, you could say, "It's tough when friends push you to do things that don't feel right." I went through similar situations when I was your age. How about we dive into some strategies that can help you respond with confidence and assertiveness?

Dealing with Common Tough Subjects

1. Talking about Mistakes: When your child makes a mistake, it's a great chance to have a chat about learning and growing instead of focusing on shame or punishment. Let us talk about this with understanding and highlight how making mistakes can lead to positive change.

For instance, if your child tells a lie, instead of getting upset, you might say, "I understand why you were worried about the consequences, but lying isn't the answer." We all make mistakes, and being honest is really important for fixing things together.

2. Dealing with Bullying: When it comes to your child being involved in bullying, whether as a victim or as someone who is bullying, it's important to have a caring and understanding conversation about it. Talk to your child about their experiences and remind them that bullying is never okay.

For instance, if your child confesses to bullying, try to stay calm and let them know you are disappointed in their actions, not in who they are as a person. Hey, you know, it really hurts when people treat others that way. I genuinely think you have it in you to show some kindness. Let's explore why this is happening and how we can fix it.

3. Talking about body image and puberty: As kids go through physical changes, they might feel a bit uncomfortable or confused about their growing bodies. Let us have open chats about body image, self-esteem, and the changes that come with puberty.

When your child shares worries about how they look, it is important to acknowledge their feelings and offer some comforting words. I get why you might be feeling a bit self-conscious right now, but just keep in mind that everyone's body is unique and has its own beauty.

Encouraging Prolonged Open Communication

Having tough conversations should not just happen once in a while. When you regularly engage in genuine conversations with your child, you lay the foundation for ongoing communication that lasts through their growing years and into adulthood. Here are a few ideas to help keep the conversation flowing:

1. **Regularly Connect:** Make it a habit to check in on how your child is feeling and what is going on in their life. This approach encourages open conversations and builds trust gradually.

2. **Stay Open:** Let your child know they can come to you anytime. Make sure to recognise how much they need help, even when things get really busy or stressful.

3. **Promote Emotional Intelligence:** Help your child learn to recognise and express their emotions, so they feel confident talking about their feelings openly.

Final Thought

Having tough talks is a big part of being a parent. They offer chances for personal growth, learning new things, and strengthening the bond between parents and kids. If parents tackle these conversations with kindness, honesty, and a good understanding of emotions, they can really help their kids face life's challenges with confidence and strength. Just keep in mind that it's not about having all the answers. It's really about creating a safe and supportive space for your child to explore their feelings and experiences.

VIII
The Significance of Empathy in Parenting

When it comes to being a good parent, empathy is key. It involves being able to understand and empathise with another person's feelings, especially those of one's own child. A parent's ability to empathise with their child's experiences helps them develop emotional intelligence, trust, and a stronger bond with their child. In this chapter, we will explore how empathy can change the way you parent, help you connect with your child on a deeper level, and influence their growth and development for the better.

What Empathy Is All About?

To truly understand and share another person's emotional experiences is the essence of empathy, which goes beyond simple kindness or sympathy. There are essentially three parts to empathy:

1. Cognitive Empathy: The ability to understand and share another person's emotional and mental state.

2. Emotional Empathy: Feeling what another person is feeling and developing a genuine connection with them on an emotional level.

3. compassionate empathy entails doing more than just feeling sorry for someone; it also means being ready to help out when asked.

Being empathetic means paying attention to how a child is feeling and reacting in a way that confirms those feelings. In addition to helping kids develop their emotional intelligence, this type of connection strengthens relationships and fosters trust.

Understanding the Importance of Empathy for Parents

When kids learn to empathise with others, they gain the confidence to stand up for themselves. Children are more likely to confide, speak honestly, and follow parental advice when they feel their parents understand and care about them. As a model of emotional intelligence, parents who are empathetic help their children develop the skills they need to manage their emotions and relationships well.

Being an empathetic parent has many benefits, including:

1. Strengthened Bonds Between Parents and Children: When parents show empathy for their children, it helps children feel safe and understood.

2. Effective Emotion Regulation: When parents show empathy, they help their children learn to control their emotions by making them feel supported instead of judged.

3. Conflict resolution: empathic parents are better able to resolve conflicts by listening to and understanding their children's perspectives while also taking into account their own feelings.

4. Improved Conduct: Children are more likely to display positive conduct when they experience emotional connection and understanding. Because they know they can express themselves positively, they are less likely to act out.

How to Develop Empathy as a Parent

1. Make an unbiased effort to listen

The first step in being an empathetic parent is to listen to your child out without making assumptions or providing answers too soon. The key is to let your kid finish expressing themselves emotionally before you react. By doing so, you show that you are open to hearing and understanding their point of view.

If your child comes home crying after a fight with a friend, you might say something like, "It seems that what your friend said has really hurt you," rather than offering solutions or advice right away. Give more details about what happened.By taking this tack, you can help your child feel safe enough to share how they really feel without worrying that others will judge them.

2. Appreciate How They Feel

Integral to empathy is the ability to validate. When parents affirm their child's feelings, they show that it is okay to feel all kinds of emotions, including happy, sad, frustrated, and scared. Recognising the genuineness and importance of the child's emotions is what we mean when we say "validation," which does not mean we agree with everything the child says or feels.

Instructions for Execution:

Use expressions like, "I get it. I understand how you feel." or "It is okay to be sad."

No matter how insignificant you think the issue is, you should never minimise or disregard their feelings. Saying something like, "It is insignificant, merely a toy," to a child who is upset because a beloved toy broke might diminish their feelings. Saying something like, "I understand how you feel, I really do. When something you hold dear breaks, it can be quite distressing.

3. Put Yourself in Your Child's Shoes

To show empathy, you must make an effort to understand your child's point of view, no matter how difficult it may be. To do this, you can try to put yourself in your child's shoes or think back on your own childhood memories. By putting yourself in your child's shoes, you can better understand their emotions and react compassionately, rather than frustrated, to their behaviour.

Refrain from becoming angry if your child is having a tantrum because they will not leave the park, for instance. Try to see things from their perspective instead. They were probably having a good time and are sad to be leaving. Saying something like, "I understand that you are enjoying your time and finding it tough to depart, but we must return home now," can show that you understand their emotions and help defuse the situation.

4. Show Compassionate Actions

Being empathetic as a parent involves more than just understanding your child's feelings; it also involves acting compassionately. Offering comfort, encouragement, and practical help when needed is part of this. By responding with empathy, you show your child that you care about how they are feeling and are willing to help them work through difficult emotions.

When your child is struggling to finish their homework and feels overwhelmed, it is not helpful to just tell them, "You must complete it.""It appears you are experiencing frustration," you can say to offer assistance instead. The best way for me to help you is to listen carefully. How about we take a break or continue working on it together?This type of response demonstrates understanding and helps your child learn to cope with difficult situations by providing them with resources and encouraging them to work together to find solutions.

The Impact of Empathy on the Growth of Children

Kids who grow up in caring homes are more likely to be emotionally stable, resilient, and good at making friends. In addition to developing empathy, they learn to recognise and control their own emotions. Empathetic parenting has several specific benefits for development, including the following:

1. **Improved Emotional Intelligence:** Kids whose parents show them empathy are more likely to be emotionally intelligent. A crucial first step in mastering emotional regulation is learning to recognise and name one's own emotions. When kids have high emotional intelligence, they are better able to handle social situations and form deep bonds with their classmates.

2. **better coping mechanisms:** Parents teach their children good coping mechanisms by showing empathy when they are going through tough times. Children learn healthy ways to express themselves emotionally rather than isolating themselves or acting impulsively when they are upset. As a result, they become more resilient and capable of facing future obstacles head-on.

3. **Understand and appriciate:** a heightened sense of self-worth develops in children whose parents make them feel understood and appreciated. They are self-aware enough to know that their emotions matter and strong enough to handle complicated emotions. All areas of their lives, from schoolwork to interpersonal relationships, benefit from this increased self-confidence.

4. **Enhanced Empathy Towards Others:** Kids whose parents are compassionate are more likely to be compassionate themselves. After receiving the same kind of encouragement from their parents, they understand the value of listening, validating, and supporting those in their immediate vicinity. Friendships, family ties, and performance in group settings (like the office or classroom) can all benefit from this empathy tendency.

Triumphing Over Obstacles to Fostering Empathetic Parenting

Being empathetic is a powerful tool for parents, but it is not always easy to keep up, especially when things get tough. Being human means that parents will always face times when it is hard to be patient or understanding. Some ways to keep empathy alive in the face of hardship are these:

1. Practice Self-Compassion: Being a parent is no easy feat, and it is normal to feel frustrated or overwhelmed from time to time. Consider practicing self-compassion when you encounter difficulties in maintaining empathy. Just keep in mind that it is okay to make mistakes and that you can learn and improve from them every day. Taking care of yourself emotionally will allow you to respond to your child with more empathy.
It is okay to step away from a situation for a while to collect your thoughts if you feel overwhelmed or angry.

2. Give Yourself a Break When You Need It: By stepping away for a moment, you can control your emotions and come back to the conversation with more empathy and clarity. Tell your kid you need a little time to gather your thoughts and that you will pick up the conversation again when you are ready.

3. Reflect on Your Childhood: Think back on your formative years and how your parents handled your emotions. Have you ever experienced feeling ignored or misunderstood? Looking back on your experiences can help you understand and relate to your child's feelings, which in turn can help you break bad habits. It can also help you improve your parenting style.

Creating a Home That Values Empathy

Creating a home that prioritises empathy goes beyond just having meaningful conversations with your child. It means creating a family atmosphere where every member feels valued, appreciated, and respected. In order to foster an empathetic atmosphere at home, consider the following:

1. Show Compassion Towards Other Family Members: Kids learn a lot by seeing how their parents interact with each other and everyone in the family. Listen attentively, acknowledge their feelings, and react compassionately to show that you care about your partner, siblings, and extended family.

2. Promote Sibling Empathy: If you have more than one child, you should encourage them to be kind to each other. Help them understand their sibling's perspective and come up with solutions that take everyone's feelings into account when arguments emerge.

3. Foster cordial environment: piece of advice is to check in with your family members on a regular basis to see how they are doing emotionally. By highlighting the significance of everyone's emotions, these check-ins foster an environment that is hospitable to openly sharing feelings. More than that, they make sure that everyone in the family learns to be compassionate.

Final Thought

When it comes to creating a nurturing, emotionally intelligent home, empathy is a powerful tool. Incorporate empathy into your everyday interactions with your child to strengthen your bond, encourage emotional development, and teach them important life skills. Staying present, attentive, and receptive are all that are required of empathy—not perfection or knowing all the answers.

IX
Discipline with Love and Logic

Parents face a big problem when they are trying to raise kids who are responsible, respectful, and emotionally smart. It is very important to find the right balance between discipline, love, and understanding. Traditional methods often use harsh punishments, which creates fear and hostility. Effective discipline, on the other hand, comes from showing love and guidance, which helps kids make better choices while keeping their sense of safety and self-esteem.

This chapter goes into more detail about the idea of using love and logic to discipline, combining understanding with clear rules that encourage responsible behaviour. It looks at ways to get kids to work together and be responsible, so that discipline is a positive, growth-promoting experience for them.

Why discipline is important?

Before getting into strategies, it is important to explain why discipline is important. Many parents think of discipline as punishment, but the word "discipline" comes from the Latin word "disciplina", which means "teaching" or "instruction."The point of discipline is not to control or punish kids, but to teach them how to control their behaviour, make smart decisions, and understand what will happen if they do something wrong.

1. Develop a sense of responsibility: Discipline helps kids see the results of their actions, both good and bad, which develops a sense of responsibility and accountability.

2. Teach Self-Control: Setting clear rules and expectations through discipline helps kids learn how to control their feelings and impulses.

3. Help kids figure out how to solve problems: Good discipline gets kids to think about their actions and come up with ways to deal with problems, instead of just following the rules out of fear.

4. Build respect: Discipline taught with love and respect teaches kids to value themselves and others.

5. Raise Emotional Intelligence: Rules and empathy help kids understand their own feelings and the feelings of others, which builds emotional intelligence.

A Balanced Look at Love and Logic

The "Love and Logic" parenting style stresses how important it is to have clear, consistent boundaries along with warmth and empathy. The founders of this philosophy were Charles Fay and Foster Cline. It teaches parents how to teach their kids to be responsible without using punishments or being strict. The idea behind love and logic parenting is based on two main ideas:

1. Empathy: Parents who show empathy for their child's feelings instead of getting angry or frustrated when they misbehave. So, even though the child is facing consequences, this makes you feel like you understand and support them.

2. Logical Consequences: Instead of punishing kids for no reason, parents let them deal with the natural or logical results of their actions. This teaches kids that the choices they make have real effects, which helps them remember important lessons.

Combining empathy with consequences not only helps kids feel loved and supported, but it also gives them the skills they need to do well in life.

Why empathy is important in disciplinary actions?

Empathy is an important part of discipline because it lets you understand how your child feels without allowing bad behaviour. Anger, frustration, sadness, or disappointment are some of the strong emotions that kids often deal with when they act out. When you show empathy, you acknowledge these feelings, which can help calm things down and make the child more willing to learn from their mistakes.

As an example: If your kid throws a fit because they do not want to stop playing video games, you could tell them, "I understand how upset you are;

you were having fun and do not want to stop." It is hard to stop doing something that makes you happy. Recognising how they feel shows that you care about their feelings while still sticking to the rule that screen time is over.

Punishments vs. Reasonable Consequences

One big difference between punishments and rational consequences is that rational consequences are based on what the child did and are meant to teach, not hurt. On the other hand, punishments do not always have anything to do with the bad behaviour and can make people angry or defiant.

An example of a punishment: When a child does not do their homework, their parent takes away their TV privileges for a week. The child might think this punishment is unfair since it has nothing to do with the homework. Instead of learning to be responsible with their homework, the child may focus on how mean their parent seems for not letting them watch TV.

An example of a logical consequence is this: The consequence for a child not doing their homework is to stay inside during playtime to finish it. This result is a direct match for the behaviour and reinforces the idea that schoolwork is important and needs to be done before fun activities. The child is more likely to understand the link between their action (forgetting to do their homework) and the result (not going to playtime), which leads to a better understanding.

Setting Clear Goals and Conditions

For kids to feel safe and protected, they need limits. Setting clear, unwavering limits helps kids know what is expected of them and what will happen if they do not do what is asked of them. Setting limits is not about controlling people; it is about teaching them how to behave responsibly and with respect in public.

The following suggestions will help you set clear boundaries:

1. Be Clear and Consistent: Make sure your child knows the rules and what will happen if they are broken. Being consistent is very important. If you change the rules a lot or do not enforce the consequences properly, it can confuse the kids or make them want to test the limits.

2. Make the Rules Fit the Child's Age: The rules you set for your child should fit his or her age and stage of development. It works best for younger kids to have clear rules and immediate consequences. As kids get older, they can handle rules with more details and consequences that happen later.

3. Explain the Reason: When kids comprehend the reasoning behind rules, they are more likely to follow them. Spend some time explaining the rationale behind the rules and why particular actions are not acceptable.

4. Allow for Adaptability: Although consistency is essential, it is also critical to recognise that there might be situations in which flexibility is required. Because life is unpredictable, rules may need to be modified in response to changing conditions.

For example, it might be reasonable to allow your child to take a short TV break before starting homework if your policy requires that homework be finished before watching TV but they have had an especially demanding day at school. This adaptability upholds the general expectation of finishing homework while exhibiting empathy.

The Importance of Regular Enforcement

Implementing consequences is one of the most difficult parts of discipline. Youngsters quickly recognise when their parents' warnings are unfounded, and they may continue to push boundaries if they believe there will not be any real consequences for their behaviour. Reliable enforcement helps kids develop a sense of responsibility by showing them that their actions have predictable results.

Advice on how to do follow-through well:

1. Keep your cool: When giving consequences, try to stay calm and collected. Showing anger or irritation can make things worse and make it harder for your child to learn from what happened.

2. Make sure there is fairness: Make sure that the consequences are fair and fit the behaviour. It is possible that harsh consequences will make you feel punished and indignant.

3. Use Natural Consequences: Let your child deal with the natural results of their actions as much as possible. For example, they will feel cold if they choose not to wear a coat on a cold day. This naturally occurring result is a powerful chance to learn.

4. Stay out of power struggles: You and your child should not turn discipline into a power struggle. Instead, show the child's consequences as results of the choices they make, not as rules they have to follow. Like, "You opted not to tidy up your toys; hence you will not have access to them tomorrow."

Teaching How to Solve Problems

Developing kids' ability to solve problems is an important part of discipline. Instead of just telling your child what they did wrong, talk to them about how they could handle similar situations better in the future. This method gives kids the power to be responsible for their actions and helps them learn how to make better decisions in the future.

Such as If there is a fight between your child and a sibling, you could say, "It looks like both you and your brothers were very upset," instead of punishing them for fighting. Let us talk about what happened. How could you handle this differently next time to avoid a fight?" This method encourages your child to think critically and helps them get better at resolving conflicts.

Strength and Self-Esteem

One problem with traditional punishment is that it can make a child feel bad about their own self-worth. Harsh punishments or constant scolding can make a child feel like they are not good enough or important. On the other hand, discipline that is based on empathy and fair consequences helps kids learn from their mistakes without making them feel like their worth is in danger.

Important Things to Do to Keep Your Self-Esteem High in Discipline:

1. Separate Behaviour from the Child: Make it clear that the behaviour, not the child as a person, is what is wrong. Say things like, "I love you, but I do not like how you are acting right now," to show that your love for your child is constant.

2. Recognise Effort: Even when you are talking to your child about bad behaviour, acknowledge the things they are trying to do. If they made a mistake but were trying to do the right thing, you should recognise that. This makes them more driven to make progress.

3. Encourage Thought: After a behaviour problem, tell your child to think about what they learnt and how they can use what they have learnt in the future. That makes the idea stronger that mistakes are chances to get better, not flaws.

Final thought

Discipline that is based on compassion and logic goes beyond just following the rules; it also teaches kids the skills they need to grow up to be responsible, emotionally intelligent, and independent adults. Parents can create a caring and supportive environment where discipline is part of personal growth and not a source of conflict by combining empathy with clear rules and logical outcomes.

X
Cultivating Autonomy and Self-Assurance

One of the best things about being a parent is seeing your kids become more independent and sure of them as they grow up. Developing these traits, however, requires careful guidance and a willingness to let kids take risks, make mistakes, and learn from their learning experiences. To encourage autonomy, you do not have to completely pull away from your kids. Instead, you can give them the tools and support they need to make choices, face challenges, and build a strong sense of self-esteem.

For kids from toddlers to teens, this chapter talks about practical ways to help them become more independent and confident while still keeping a safe and caring environment.

What Does Autonomy Mean?

Autonomy is important for a child's overall growth because it helps them:

1. Building Self-Esteem: Giving kids the chance to take responsibility for their actions and themselves builds their confidence in their abilities.

2. Improving Problem-Solving Skills: Giving kids freedom lets them face problems and think about how to solve them on their own, which encourages creativity and persistence.

3. Improving the ability to make decisions: When kids have to make choices, they learn how to weigh their options, think about what might happen, and take responsibility for their choices.

4. Teaching Accountability: Giving kids freedom also gives them a sense of responsibility by showing them the link between what they do and what happens.

5. Getting ready for adulthood: promoting independence is an important step towards becoming an adult, where being able to make your own decisions and be self-sufficient are key to success in both personal and professional life.

Finding the Right Balance Between Help and Freedom

The most important thing about encouraging independence is finding a good balance between helping your child and giving them room to learn and grow. Overprotecting a child can make it harder for them to develop independence, while giving them too much freedom without any guidance can make them feel unsafe or make bad choices. Here are some ways to find that balance:

1. Push for age-appropriate independence: You should gradually encourage your child to become independent in a way that fits their age and level of development. For example, you can give toddler choices about what to wear, and you can give a teenager responsibility for their schoolwork.

2. Do not be afraid of making mistakes: They are an important part of learning. When kids face disappointment or failure, it gives them a chance to figure out what went wrong and build resilience. Refrain from fixing their problems right away or protecting them from failing. Instead, offer support and direction as they face problems.

3. Give your child choices: Giving your child choices encourages independence and gives them a sense of power. . For younger children, offer restricted choices to avert overwhelming them.. As they get older, give them more complicated choices that let them practise weighing pros and cons.

4. Set a good example of autonomy: kids learn a lot from watching their parents. Show independent behaviour by showing that you can solve problems, make decisions, and take care of yourself in your own life. Show how you deal with problems and take responsibility for what you do.

5. Raise your child's responsibilities gradually: As they get older, raise their responsibilities gradually. Start with small tasks, like setting the table or organising the kids' toys, and work your way up to bigger ones, like managing the money, taking care of younger siblings, or helping with housework.

Getting more confident by using positive reinforcement
Having confidence is a key part of becoming independent. Children need to believe in their own abilities to make decisions and deal with problems. Giving yourself positive feedback is a good way to boost your confidence.
1. Recognise work, not just results: Instead of only focussing on the end result, praise the work your child puts in. This method helps them see that working hard and not giving up is more important than being perfect. For example: when your child tries new activity praise their effort and bravery instead of just checking to see if they succeeded.
2. Encourage a Growth Mindset: To encourage a growth mindset in kids, you need to teach them that they can improve their skills and intelligence by working hard and learning new things. Help your kid understand that making mistakes is a way to learn and that facing challenges makes them stronger. As they learn, help them see setbacks as normal parts of the process.
3. Be Wary of Too Much Praise: It is important to boost your confidence, but it is also important to be wary of praise that is too much or not sincere. Kids can tell when praise is not sincere, and giving too much praise can make them feel like they have to always do well. Instead, give specific, sincere praise that shows you notice real effort and progress.
4. Celebrate small victories: Celebrate small wins, even if they do not seem important, to boost your confidence. Every step towards independence is worth celebrating, no matter how small it is. This activity helps kids see how far they have come and feel proud of what they have done.

Teaching How to Solve Problems Well
Problem-solving is one of the most important life skills that kids need to become independent. Kids gain confidence in their ability to handle new challenges when they can think critically and come up with solutions on their own. You can help them get better at this skill in the following ways:
1. **Ask Open-Ended Questions:** Do not give your child the answer right away; instead, ask them questions that make them think critically. For example, if they are having trouble with a task, ask, "What do you think you could do next?" or "How can we work together to solve this problem?"
2. Break Problems Down into Smaller, More Doable Steps: Teach your child how to break down big problems into smaller, more doable steps. This method makes problem-solving less overwhelming and gives them a structured plan for what to do next.

3. Encourage Brainstorming: When your child is faced with a problem, tell them to think of more than one way to solve it. It is easier to think creatively and consider different points of view when you do this activity.

4. Give Your Child Chances to Solve Problems: Give your child chances to solve problems in real life. This could mean planning an activity, managing their time, or dealing with a disagreement with a peer. The more often they do these kinds of things, the more confident they will become in their abilities.

Encouraging Decision-Making
Facilitating Decision-Making Processes

Making choices is an important part of being autonomous. It is very important for kids to be able to make decisions and understand what those decisions mean. Here are some things you can do to help them learn how to make good decisions:

1. Start with Simple Choices: For younger people, give them simple choices like picking out clothes, picking out a snack, or picking out a book to read. In a low-stress environment, this helps them get better at making decisions.

2. Think about the possibilities of what might happen: As kids get older, talk to them about what might happen if they make a choice. Help them think about both the good and bad outcomes of their choices, which will help them make more thoughtful decisions.

3. Accept Mistakes: Let your child deal with the results of their choices, even if that means making mistakes. It is usually a good idea to let them learn from the experience if the decision does not have any big effects. This helps them understand what it means to be responsible and makes them more thoughtful about the choices they make.

4. Encourage reflection: After making a choice and then experiencing its results, you should encourage your child to think back on the process. Pose inquiries such as, "What aspects do you believe transpired effectively?" or "How might you approach this differently in the future?" This practice of reflecting helps you remember what you have learnt and encourages a growth mindset.

Giving up control and trusting your child

Because your child is becoming more independent, it may be hard for you to give up control and let them make their own choices. It is natural to want to protect them from harm or disappointment, but being too protective can stop them from becoming independent and confident.

1. Believe in the Journey: Remember that becoming independent is a process that takes time, and your child will need time to learn the skills they need. Believe that they will learn from their mistakes, even if they have to make them along the way.

2. Be a supportive safety net: It is important to give your child room to grow, but they should always know that you are there for them if they need help. Assure them that they can come to you for help or advice whenever they need to, but have faith in their ability to handle things on their own.

3. Look at failures as chances to learn: Your child will learn more from setbacks if you help them see them as learning opportunities. This point of view makes them less afraid of failing and more willing to take risks and try new things.

4. Honour Their Independence: As your child starts to become independent, be proud of their progress and what they have done. Recognise their achievements and let them know how proud you are of what they have done. This positive feedback makes them feel better about their abilities.

Final thought

Giving your child the tools they need to be independent and confident is a great gift you can give them. By letting them make choices, solve problems, and take on responsibility, you give them the tools they need to face the world with confidence and resilience. You may find it hard to let go of control sometimes, but trusting your child to grow and learn will help them become skilled, confident, and independent adults.

As parents, we do not want to protect our kids from all problems, but we do want to give them the tools they need to deal with the world on their own terms. Giving kids the freedom to explore, careful guidance, and positive reinforcement can help them build the independence and confidence they need to do well.

XI

Navigating Peer Pressure and Social Influences

Growing up and spending more time with their peers' exposes kids to different social influences that can change their behaviour, values, and sense of who they are. Especially peer pressure has a strong effect on kids' choices and can sometimes lead them down paths that go against what they were taught or what they believe. Successfully navigating this terrain necessitates a solid foundation in self-awareness, confidence, and communication, all of which can be cultivated through attentive parenting. This chapter goes into detail about how to understand peer pressure, tell the difference between the good and bad effects of social influences, and give kids the tools they need to make their own responsible decisions.

Being able to handle peer pressure

Peer pressure happens when kids feel like they have to follow the rules, values, or expectations of their friends. It can show up directly, like when a friend encourages them to try something new, or indirectly, like when they feel pressured just by watching how other people act. Peer pressure can affect choices in both good and bad ways, and it is important for kids to learn how to deal with these situations as they get older.

Different Kinds of Peer Pressure:

1. **Positive Peer Pressure:** Not all pressure from peers is bad. Positive peer pressure happens when kids' friends encourage them to make healthy choices, do good things, or work on themselves. A group of friends, for

example, might push a child to do well in school, play sports, or do good things for other people.

2. Bad Peer Pressure: This is when people push each other to do or make decisions that go against their values or good sense. This could mean trying out risky behaviours like drug abuse, bullying, or skipping school.

Peer pressure makes kids give in for these reasons:

1. Wanting Acceptance: Kids, especially teens, want to be accepted and feel like they belong. Peer pressure may make them think that conforming to expectations is necessary to fit in, avoid rejection, or keep friendships.

2. Fear of Being Left Out: The fear of being left out or laughed at can be a strong motivator for kids to do what others want, even if it makes them feel bad.

3. Curiosity: Sometimes, peer pressure can make a child want to try new things or find something new. This allure can be especially strong in places where trying new things is seen as cool, like when people try alcohol or vape.

4. Lack of confidence: Kids who do not trust their own judgement or who are not sure of who they are may be more likely to give in to peer pressure. They might question their gut feelings and let other people tell them what to do.

Teaching kids how to spot and avoid harmful influences

That is why it takes time to develop the skill of being able to spot and resist negative peer pressure. Parents are very important in helping their kids develop the awareness, self-confidence, and decision-making skills they need to deal with stress in a healthy way.

1. Boosting your confidence and self-assurance

Building a strong sense of self-worth is one of the best ways to give kids the strength to stand up to negative peer pressure. When kids have a good opinion of themselves and believe in what they believe in, they are less likely to give in to outside influences.

2. Encourage self-reflection by: Help your child think about their strengths, values, and what makes them special. Being self-aware gives them confidence and helps them figure out what is important to them, even when other people are pressuring them to do something else.

3. Verify What They are Worth: Remind your child of their worth by noticing their good qualities, accomplishments, and efforts on a regular basis. Tell them that their thoughts and feelings are important and that you value them for who they really are, not how well they fit in with social norms.

4. Show Confidence: Kids often copy what they see others do. Show that you have faith in your own choices and values, even when you are in a tough social situation. Tell me about times in your life when you stood up for yourself or did something different for a good reason.

Teaching people how to think critically

Getting better at critical thinking is one of the most important things you can do to fight negative peer pressure. Kids need to be able to look at situations, weigh the risks, and make choices based on their own thoughts, not just what other people say.

1. Instill Consequence Analysis: Tell your child to think about what might happen if they do something. Ask them things like, "What might happen if you choose that path?" or "How might you feel about this choice in the future?"

2. Thought Out Scenarios: Play pretend with your child or talk about possible situations where they might face peer pressure. Learn about different ways to respond and help them get better at saying "no" with confidence.

3. Encourage Questioning and Care: Tell your child to think about what their friends do and the latest trends instead of just going along with it. Teaching them to ask, "Why do people act in this way?" or "Is this choice in line with my values?" encourages them to make decisions on their own.

Teaching kids how to get along with others

Kids often give in to peer pressure because they are not good at setting limits or letting others know when they are uncomfortable in social situations. Giving them strong social skills can help them handle these kinds of situations more easily.

1. Encourage Being Assertive: Help your child get better at stating their opinions and setting limits without getting violent. Sayings like "No, thank you," "That is not okay with me," or "I have other things I need to do" are short but powerful ways to stand firm.

2. Encourage good relationships: Peer pressure is less likely to happen in relationships based on mutual respect, trust, and shared values. Tell your kid to look for friends who will support their decisions and help them feel good about themselves.

3. Help with dealing with peer rejection: Refusing to give in to peer pressure can sometimes lead to temporary exclusion or conflict. Teach your child that it is okay if not everyone agrees with them and that real friends will respect their boundaries. They can also get better prepared by acting out how they would react if a peer rejected them.

How to Deal with Online Peer Pressure and Social Media

In today's digital world, peer pressure goes beyond face-to-face interactions. Social media makes social influences stronger, creating an atmosphere where teens feel like they have to present a certain image, follow popular trends, or compare themselves to their peers. Getting around in this digital world adds a new level of difficulty to dealing with peer pressure.

1. Teaching how to use technology well

Teach your kids about the carefully constructed facade that is common on social media. Make it easier for them to understand that the internet often shows a skewed version of reality, with people posting things to get approval instead of being themselves.

- **Find out what "Likes" and "Comments" Really Mean:** You should talk to your child about how the need for approval through likes, comments, and followers can lead to more harmful peer pressure. Instead of following the latest trend, they should push for the creation of content that is true to their own interests and values.
- **Set limits on how you can use social media:** Set rules and regulations for how people can use social media, like limiting screen time, encouraging short breaks from digital platforms, and keeping an eye on what people do online. Setting healthy limits for your child on social media can help them grow up with a well-rounded view of its effects.

2. Encouraging Posts With Thought

You should tell your child to be careful about what they say online. Before they share, ask them, "Will this make me proud in the future?" and "How does this fit with my values?" Learn more about the idea of digital footprints. It is important for your child to know that what they do online leaves a digital trail that can have long-lasting effects. Remind them that their online content can be looked at by many people, such as potential employers, teachers, and other groups.

- **Support online communities that are positive:** Encourage your child to look for online groups or forums that share their interests and values. Instead of encouraging harmful peer pressure, good digital environments can encourage creativity, make learning easier, and speed up personal growth.
- **Peer pressure and adolescence: The Most Important Years** You are most likely to give in to peer pressure when you are a teenager, because that is when you start to look for more independence and make your own social identity. As teens try to figure out who they are, they may be more likely to do risky things and give in to outside influences at this point.

3. Open communication is very important

When a person hits puberty, keeping lines of communication open becomes significantly more important. It is very important to create a safe space where your teen feels comfortable talking about their experiences, worries, and problems.

- **Trying Not to Judge Too Quickly:** Parents, when your child talks about tough situations or problems with other kids, do not criticise or punish them right away. Actively listen and offer advice without making them feel bad about themselves.
- **As a Source You Can Trust:** Make sure your child knows they can come to you for advice or help if they ever feel stressed or unsure about something. If you present yourself as a reliable source, people will be more likely to look to you for advice before making important choices.

4. Help people take healthy risks

Being a teenager means naturally wanting to take risks, which is an important part of growing up. Do not just try to keep your child from doing dangerous things. Instead, guide them towards activities that involve positive risks that will help them learn and grow.

- **Putting their energy into being productive:** Encourage children to get involved in activities like sports, arts, community service, or business, where they can take risks, push themselves, and enjoy the feeling of success without worrying about what might happen.

- **Taking Care of Their Freedom:** Adolescents want to be independent, but they need your help. Help them find the right balance between freedom and responsibility by letting them explore and available to help when needed.

Final thought

Teenagers and young adults will always have to deal with peer pressure, but with the right tools and help, they can handle social influences in a way that fits with their values and personal growth. By helping their kids build self-confidence, critical thinking skills, and good social skills, parents can give them the tools they need to be strong enough to make their own decisions, even when other kids are pressuring them.

In the end, the goal is to give kids the confidence to stick to their beliefs, the smarts to spot outside influences, and the social skills to stand up for themselves with poise and confidence.

XII
Cultivating Emotional Intelligence in Children

Emotional intelligence (EI) is the skill of being able to understand, control, and express your feelings, as well as relate to others. It is an important part of a child's overall development and will affect their relationships, how well they do in school, and how they interact with others in the future. This chapter will talk about why emotional intelligence is important, how it affects different parts of life, and some useful ways to help kids develop EI.

Why emotional intelligence is important?
Emotional intelligence is more than just controlling your own feelings. It also means being able to read other people's feelings and react in the right way. This set of skills helps kids deal with problems, make better choices, and understand how to interact with others. Many research projects have found that kids who are emotionally smart are more likely to:

- **Have Better Academic Performance:** Being emotionally intelligent helps kids stay focused, deal with stress, and work well with others, all of which lead to better school performance.
- **Build stronger relationships:** Kids who have a high level of EI are better at talking about how they feel, solving problems, and seeing things from other people's points of view. Because of this, friendships and relationships get better over time.

- **Deal with Stress and Problems:** Emotional intelligence gives kids the skills they need to deal with bad feelings, get through tough times, and bounce back from setbacks.
- **Make Responsible Choices:** Being emotionally aware helps kids think about what will happen if they do something and help them make better, more caring choices.

Important Parts of Emotional Intelligence

There are several important parts that make up emotional intelligence and all of them help a child control their feelings and get along with others:

1. **Self-awareness**: being able to see and understand your own feelings.

2. **Self-Regulation:** Being able to handle and control your emotions, especially when things are tough.

3. **Motivation:** the drive to reach your goals, even when things go wrong or you feel bad.

4. **Empathy:** the skill of being able to understand and share another person's feelings and then respond to them in a kind way.

5. **Social skills:** being able to make and keep healthy relationships, work out disagreements, and talk to people clearly.

How to Improve Your Emotional Intelligence Everyday

Emotional intelligence starts in the home, where kids learn how to deal with and talk about their feelings. Parents are very important for teaching their kids how to be emotionally intelligent and making sure they have a safe place to talk about their feelings. Here are some ways to help kids develop their emotional intelligence.

1. Encourage people to show their feelings

Kids should be able to talk about how they feel, whether they are scared, happy, angry, or frustrated. Assisting kids in expressing their emotions helps them learn more about themselves and improves their communication skills.

- **Label Emotions:** Help your child figure out what they are feeling and what it means. Say something like, "It looks like you are feeling frustrated," instead of ignoring how they feel. Would you like to talk about it?" Labelling emotions helps people find the words to describe what they are feeling.

- **Normalise All Feelings:** Always remind your child that all feelings, good or bad, are okay and normal. Do not call feelings like sadness or anger "bad." Instead, help your child understand that these feelings are normal and that there are healthy ways to deal with them.
- **Make a Safe Space:** Give your child a place where they can talk about their feelings without worrying about being judged or punished. Say things like, "I understand why you are feeling this way," to show that you understand how they feel when they are upset.

2. Show how to use emotional intelligence

Kids learn how to control their feelings by watching how the adults in their lives deal with tough situations. Showing them how to use emotional intelligence teaches them how to handle problems with self-control and understanding.

- **Take Charge of Your Emotions:** Show others healthy ways to deal with their stress, anger, or frustration. Saying something like, "I am really angry right now, so let me take a deep breath before we talk about this" can help you calm down.
- **Use Empathy in Your Conversations:** Show empathy in the way you talk to other people every day. Your child will learn how important it is to be kind and understanding if they see you being that way. You could say, "It looks like your friend is upset." What do you think we could do to make them feel better?"
- **Talk About Your Feelings:** Be honest with your child about how you are feeling. Tell them that adults also feel a lot of different things. These things teach kids that having feelings is okay, and they make them more likely to talk about their own.

3. Teach ways to control yourself

It is not enough to just be aware of your emotions; you need to be able to control them too. Kids need help learning how to control their feelings, especially when things are too much or stressful.

- **Instructions on How to Breathe:** Show your kid easy ways to calm down when they are upset. Taking slow, deep breaths can help them calm down and get their emotions under control. Tell them to do these things over and over again until they become automatic.

- **Use a "Pause" button:** Teach your kid to take a moment to calm down before acting out. For example, you could tell them to count to ten before they speak when they are angry. This gives them time to think about how they feel and what they want to do.
- **Problem-Solving:** When your child is angry or frustrated, help them figure out how to solve their problem. Ask them, "What do you think we could do to make this situation better?" instead of focussing on how they feel. Problem-solving teaches them to think about how to solve problems instead of dwelling on their feelings.

4. Build empathy

Empathy is an important part of emotional intelligence because it helps kids connect with others more deeply and treat others with kindness. Teaching kids empathy makes them more caring and helps them form stronger relationships.

- **Perspective-taking:** Tell your kid to imagine what other people might be feeling in different situations. "How do you think that made your friend feel?" is a question that you could ask. "What do you think we should do to help them feel better?"
- **Read books about emotions:** Stories are a great way for kids to learn about different feelings and points of view. Ask your child to pick out books with characters who are having emotional problems and to describe how they feel or what they could do differently.
- **Do Kind Things:** Tell your kid to do kind things, like helping a friend, being there for a sibling, or doing community service. These things help kids learn to care about others and understand how their actions can affect other people.

5. Learn how to get along with others

Kids who have good social skills can get along better with others, make real connections, and handle conflicts better. Social skills and emotional intelligence go hand in hand. As kids learn to talk about their needs and meet the needs of others, they develop their emotional intelligence.

- **Help Your Child Work Together:** Let your child work with others by doing group projects, playing sports with other kids, or just playing together. Cooperation is a good way for kids to learn how to talk to each other, make deals, and work together.
- **Teach Your Child How to Handle Conflicts:** When disagreements happen, show your child how to settle them without violence. Show them how to respectfully share their feelings, listen to the other person, and work together to find a solution.
- **Praise Good Behaviour:** When your child shows empathy, cooperation, or kindness, let them know you noticed. To encourage good social interactions, praise specific actions, like "I loved how you helped your friend when they were sad."

Emotional intelligence and doing well in school

Developing emotional intelligence can have a big effect on how well a child does in school. Kids who have a high EI can handle stress better, stay focused, and get along with their peers better. Kids who are emotionally intelligent:

- **Manage Test Anxiety:** Kids who know how to control their emotions can handle the stress of tests and exams better, which makes them less anxious and helps them do better.
- **Work Well with Others:** Working on projects with other people requires talking and working together, and emotional intelligence helps with both of these things. Kids who know how to work with others are more likely to do well in these kinds of school settings.
- **Deal with Feedback in a Positive Way:** Emotional intelligence helps kids take criticism in a positive way and use it to improve their work instead of getting angry or upset.

How to Raise Children Who Are Emotionally Smart

Teaching kids how to deal with their feelings is one of the best things parents can do for them. We give kids the tools they need to face the challenges of life with confidence and strength by teaching them to understand and control their emotions, understand how others feel, and build strong social skills.

Being emotionally intelligent is not something you are born with; it is a skill that you can develop with practice and help. Giving kids a safe place to talk about their feelings, acting in an emotionally intelligent way yourself, and teaching them self-control and empathy skills are all things that parents can do to raise emotionally intelligent kids who can make friends and do well in all areas of their lives.

Children who are emotionally intelligent grow up to be emotionally intelligent adults who can lead with empathy, deal with problems with grace, and make the world a better place. When we parent with emotional intelligence in mind, we help our kids have a better, more caring future.

XIII
Managing Parenting Stress with Emotional Intelligence

Being a parent is without a doubt one of the best things in the world, but it also causes a lot of stress. Parents often feel like they have too much to do between running the household and meeting their kids' emotional and physical needs. As hard as it is, they have to deal with this stress in a way that does not hurt their relationship with their kids or their health in general.

This chapter will talk about how parents can use emotional intelligence (EI) to deal with stress in a healthy way. Parents can handle the stresses of parenting more calmly and make their home a healthier place for their family by practicing self-awareness, self-regulation, empathy, and strong social skills every day.

How stress affects being a parent

Parents can feel stressed in many ways, such as being tired from juggling work and home duties, worrying about their children's future, getting angry at behaviour problems, and worrying about money, to name a few. Ignoring stress can cause:

1. Irritability and Short Temper: Stressed parents may lose their cool more easily, which can lead to frequent outbursts or fights with their kids.

2. Emotional Burnout: Long-term stress can make people emotionally tired, which makes it harder for parents to be there for their kids emotionally.

3. The relationship between parents and children gets worse: When stress takes over, parents and children often do not understand each other and feel emotionally distant from each other.

4. Bad Role Modelling: Kids learn from watching their parents. It could make them less able to handle their feelings if they see their parents constantly stressed.

Emotional intelligence gives parents tools to help them control their feelings, keep things in perspective, and respond in a healthy way even when things are hard.

Self-awareness can help you figure out what causes stress.

To deal with stress, you must first understand what causes it. Self-awareness, or being able to see and understand your own emotions, is the first step towards emotional intelligence.

How to Become More Self-Aware:

1. **Track Emotional Patterns:** Keep a journal of your feelings and write down what events or situations make you feel stressed. This will help you see patterns and figure out what makes you angry or stressed.
For instance, if you feel most stressed when your kids fight while you are making dinner, that means this time of day is especially hard for you.

2. Check in with yourself often: Ask yourself, "How am I feeling right now?" several times a day. Regularly checking in with yourself can help keep stress from getting worse.
For example, if you feel yourself getting tense in the middle of a busy morning, acknowledge that feeling and take a deep breath before you act.

3. Know the Physical Signs of Stress: Stress often shows up in our bodies before we realise it in our minds. If you feel stressed, your shoulders might feel tight, your heart might be racing, or your breathing might be shallow. When you see these signs, they mean you should slow down and think about what is going on before reacting emotionally.

Self-Regulation: Keeping your emotions in check
The next step after becoming self-aware is self-regulation, which means being able to handle and control your emotions. When parents are under a lot of stress, self-regulation helps them stop and think of a better way to respond instead of acting on impulse.

Ways to keep yourself in check:

1. The Power of the Pause: It is helpful to learn to stop and think before you act when you are feeling stressed. This short break gives you a chance to take a step back, think about what is going on, and respond with logic instead of emotion.
If your child refuses to do their homework, do not get angry right away. Instead, take a deep breath and ask them calmly why they do not want to do it. This method encourages communication instead of making things worse.

2. Breathing Exercises: Deep breathing exercises can help calm your nervous system when you are feeling stressed. Doing slow, deep breathing sets off the body's relaxation response, which makes you feel more in charge.
In a stressful situation, take four deep breaths in, hold them for four seconds, and then let them out for four seconds. This easy activity can instantly make you feel less stressed.

3. Changing the way you think about negative thoughts: It is easy to think about the worst-case scenarios or talk badly to yourself when you are stressed. When you reframe something, you look at it from a different, more positive angle.
If you feel like you are a bad parent because you can not stop your child from throwing tantrums, try this instead: "Tantrums are a normal part of child development, and I am learning how to help them deal with these feelings."

Empathy is being able to feel what other people are feeling
Empathy is a key part of emotional intelligence and a very important skill for parents to have. When you show empathy for your kids, you can better understand their emotional needs and respond in a way that builds connection instead of conflict.

How to Teach Your Kids to Feel Empathy:

1. **Try to understand what your child is going through:** When kids act out or do bad things, it is usually because they are having a hard time with their feelings. Try to see things from their point of view.
If your child refuses to go to bed, do not see it as defiance. Instead, think about the possibility that they are scared or anxious about something, like the dark or nightmares. This change in point of view lets you respond with more compassion.
2. **Validate Their Feelings:** When you validate a child's feelings, even if they seem over the top, they know that you understand and respect them.
Instead of telling your child, "It is not a big deal" when they are upset that a friend did not want to play with them at school, say, "I can see that you are hurt because your friend did not want to play with you."
3. **Active Listening:** To practise active listening, give your child your full attention when they talk about how they feel. This makes them feel cared for and heard.
You should resist the urge to interrupt or offer solutions right away when your teen is upset about school. Allow them to talk about how they feel and show that you are truly listening.

Building support networks with social skills
Developing strong social skills is another part of emotional intelligence. These skills can help parents find support, handle relationships, and talk to their kids and other people more clearly.

Getting more social support:

1. **Look for a community:** Being a parent can make you feel alone, especially when you are under a lot of stress. Getting together with other parents, family members, or friends who understand how hard it is to be a parent can give you much-needed emotional support.

For example, join a parenting group in your area or an online forum where parents can share their experiences and give you advice.

2. Talk to your partner openly: If you are co-parenting, it is important to keep the lines of communication open with your partner to deal with stress. Talk about your feelings, problems, and needs on a regular basis so that you can help each other.

Have a check-in with your partner at the end of a stressful day. Ask them how they are doing, tell them about yours, and help each other deal with the things that are stressing you out.

3. Set Boundaries: Another part of social skills is setting healthy limits, both with your kids and with other people. Setting limits prevents burnout and protects your emotional health.

For example, if you have too many things to do, it is okay to say "no" to extra requests from family, friends, or even your kids. You can be fully present when needed if you set limits on your emotions.

How to Take Care of Yourself to Deal with Stress

Self-care is not a nice-to-have; it is a must, especially for parents. When you take care of your physical, mental, and emotional health, you can be the best parent anyone could ask for.

How Parents Can Take Care of Theirself:

1. Plan "Me Time": Give yourself time every day or week to be alone. You can recharge during this time by reading, going for a walk, or doing something you enjoy for 15 minutes.

Example: Make it a habit to do something that makes you happy for 20 minutes every night after the kids are asleep. For example, you could write in a journal or stretch.

2. Do some exercise: Research has shown that exercise can help reduce stress. Whether you go for a short walk or a full workout, moving around can help you feel better and clear your mind.

Simple exercises that you can do every day include stretching while your child plays or doing a quick workout at home when you have time.

3. Mindfulness and Meditation: Mindfulness practices, like meditation, help lower stress by helping you focus and calm down.

Do a five-minute mindfulness meditation when you have a break in your day. Pay attention to your breath and let go of any thoughts that are making you feel stressed.

How to Be a Good Parent with Emotional Resilience

There will always be stressful times as a parent, but parents can build the resilience they need to handle these problems with grace if they learn emotional intelligence. Parents can not only deal with their own stress but also make their kids' lives better and healthier by being self-aware, controlling their emotions, learning empathy, and developing strong social skills.

In the next chapter, we will talk about some useful ways to teach kids how to deal with their own feelings and stress, which will help them become strong from a young age. This is a very important step in developing emotionally intelligent and self-confident kids who can handle life's challenges well.

XIV
Raising Emotionally Resilient Children

One of the best things we can do as parents is teach our kids how to deal with life's problems by being emotionally strong. Children who are emotionally resilient are better able to deal with setbacks, control their feelings, and keep a positive outlook on life in a world full of stress, uncertainty, and changes. We will talk about ways to make kids emotionally strong in this chapter, including how to teach them problem-solving and flexibility, as well as how to understand the value of emotional validation.

How to Understand Emotional Strength
Emotional resilience means being able to bounce back from problems, adjust to new situations, and keep growing even when things are hard. It gives kids the skills to deal with their feelings in a healthy way, but it does not mean they will not feel sad, angry, or worried.
Emotional resilience is not something kids are born with, according to research. It is something they build over time through good relationships, safe environments, and learning how to deal with problems. Parents are very important for teaching these skills to kids from a very young age.

Putting together a base of emotional safety
Emotional security is the first thing that makes you emotionally strong. When kids feel loved, supported, and safe with their parents, they are more likely to build the confidence and self-esteem they need to deal with

problems. Some important things you can do to help your child feel emotionally safe are:

1. Give children consistent emotional support: Kids do better in places where they feel emotionally supported. This means being there to listen, understand how they feel, and offer comfort when things are hard.

If your child is upset that they were not invited to a birthday party, do not tell them, "You will be fine." Instead, acknowledge their feelings by telling them, "I can see you are really disappointed, and it is okay to feel that way."

2. Set up a routine and make things predictable: Making things predictable in a child's daily life makes them feel safe because it gives them a sense of control over their surroundings. Routines help keep things stable, especially when things are stressful.

Example: Set up a relaxing bedtime routine that will help your child relax after a long day and make them feel safe and secure.

3. Be emotionally available: Being there matters. When kids know they can talk to you about their problems, they feel safer and more sure of how to handle their feelings.

As an example, talk to your child every day about their day and give them a safe place to talk about both the good and bad things that happened.

Teaching how to be emotionally aware and express yourself

Emotional awareness, or being able to recognise and name your feelings, is a key part of being resilient. Helping kids figure out how they feel and say what they are feeling in a healthy way helps them deal with their feelings instead of being overwhelmed by them.

Ways to Help People Understand Their Feelings:

1. Name the Emotion: While kids are feeling strong emotions, help them name what they are feeling. Kids feel understood and learn to recognise their feelings when you do this simple thing.

For example, if your child is having a temper tantrum, you could say, "It looks like you are really upset right now." "Let us talk about what is making you mad."

2. Use Emotional Words Often: Use emotional words in everyday conversation. It is easier for kids to deal with their feelings when they feel like they can talk about them.

As an example, ask everyone in the family to talk about something that made them happy, sad, or angry that day. This makes talking about feelings seem normal.

3. Encourage kids to express themselves in a variety of ways: Some kids may find it hard to talk about their feelings. Help them deal with their feelings by giving them other ways to express themselves, such as drawing, writing, or playing.

Example: If your kid is upset or angry, tell them to draw or write a letter about what is running through their mind.

Promoting the ability to solve problems and adapt

Being resilient is more than just being able to control your feelings. It also means being able to solve problems and change when things do not go as planned. Teaching kids how to think about problems with an eye towards finding solutions can help them feel strong when things get tough.

Ways to help kids learn how to solve problems:

1. Show kids how to solve problems in everyday life: Kids watch how you deal with problems and learn from that. Explain to your child how you think about problems when you face them. This will show them that you can solve them with patience and creativity.

For example, if something breaks in the house, do not get angry. Instead, calmly help your child figure out what to do. "I see that the chair is broken." "Let us work together to fix it."

2. Teach your child to think for themselves: When your child has a small problem, tell them to think of ways to solve it instead of fixing it right away.

Example: If your kid is having trouble building a tower with blocks, do not help right away. Ask, "What do you think would help make it more stable?" instead.

3. Teach kids how to be flexible and adaptable: Things do not always go as planned, so teaching kids how to deal with that is an important part of building resilience. They need to know that change is a part of life and that

it is okay to change what they expect.
If bad weather forces you to cancel a family trip, show your disappointment and then include them in planning a different, equally fun activity.

Teaching People How to Deal with Difficult Feelings

Kids who are resilient know how to deal with tough feelings without getting upset or reacting. Kids can deal with stress, anger, and anxiety in a healthy way when they know how to cope.

Effective ways to deal with stress:

1. Exercises for the lungs: Teaching kids easy breathing exercises can help them calm down when they are upset or stressed.
As an example, teach your child how to take deep breaths by having them slowly breathe in for four counts, hold their breath for four counts, and then breathe out for four counts. So they can use it when they are stressed, practise this with them when they are calm.

2. Mindfulness Practices: Being mindful helps kids stay in the present, which makes them less anxious about the future or stuck in the past.
Take your child on a "mindful walk" where you both focus on noticing all the sounds, sights, and smells around you. This makes kids more aware of their surroundings and helps them stay in the present.

3. Expressing yourself creatively: art, music, and physical activities like dancing or sports are all great ways to let out stress and emotions that have been building up.
For example, if your child is having a hard time, tell them to dance, paint, or play an instrument to calm down.

4. Positive Self-Talk: Teach your child to say positive things to them when they think something bad. Helping them create a positive internal dialogue can make them stronger when things get tough.
For instance, if your child says, "I am not good at this," tell them to say, "I am learning and getting better every time I try."

Getting people to take healthy risks

To make kids more resilient, you should also push them out of their comfort zones and encourage them to take healthy risks. When kids face problems and solve them, they feel better about their skills. They learn important lessons about persistence and hard work even when they fail.

Ways to encourage taking risks in a healthy way:
1. Give your child chances to try new things: Take them to new places, activities, and social situations where they can test their skills in a safe environment.
Example: Tell your kid to try something new, like learning to ride a bike, being in a school play, or joining a sports team. These things teach them that it can be fun to try new things, even if they are scary.

2. Praise Effort, Not Just Success: No matter what happens, praise your child for the effort they put into trying something new. They feel free to take risks because they know they will not fail.
Instead of focussing on the outcome, praise your child for their hard work and willingness to try if they compete in a race but do not win.

3. Teach Resilience through Failure: Everyone fails sometimes, and it is important to teach kids how to deal with it with grace and persistence if you want them to be resilient. Help them see that failing is a chance to get better and learn.
Use the time your child fails a test or loses a game to teach them something. Talk about what they can do better next time and what they can learn from this.

Making strong connections with other people

Kids who are resilient also make strong friendships that help them feel better. Being emotionally strong depends on having friends, family, and a sense of belonging in a community.

Ways to make people more socially resilient:

1. Support Good Relationships Between Peers: Teach your child how to make strong, healthy friendships by teaching them how to talk to others, share, and settle disagreements.
For instance, act out with your child how to talk to a new friend at school or

how to settle a disagreement in a polite way.

2. Be an Example of Empathy and Compassion: Teach your kid how to care about other people and have empathy for them. Kids are better able to handle their feelings when they feel connected and cared for.
As an example, help people in need by volunteering as a family. Giving back and caring about others are important lessons for kids to learn from this, which can help them feel like they belong and understand how others feel.

3. Encourage them to socialise: Encourage your child to join team sports, clubs, or other activities with other people. This will help them improve their social skills and learn how to work with others.
If your kid likes football, get them to join a local team where they can make friends and learn how to work together as a team.

www.ingramcontent.com/pod-product-compliance
Lightning Source LLC
Chambersburg PA
CBHW031452150726
47990CB00007B/2718